THE GIRL ON THE BEST SELLER LIST
Vin Packer

WITHDRAWN

Black Gat Books • Eureka California

THE GIRL ON THE BEST SELLER LIST

Published by Black Gat Books
A division of Stark House Press
1315 H Street
Eureka, CA 95501, USA
griffinskye3@sbcglobal.net
www.starkhousepress.com

Originally published by Gold Medal Books,
Greenwich, and copyright © 1960 by Fawcett
Publications, Inc.

Published by arrangement with Adams Media, an
F+W Media, Inc. Company, 57 Littlefield Street, Avon,
MA 02322, USA.

ISBN: 1-933586-98-2
ISBN-13: 978-1-933586-98-4

Book design by Mark Shepard, SHEPGRAPHICS.COM

First Black Gat Edition: May 2016

FIRST EDITION

One

... and the town sat in the lush hills of the Finger Lakes, sat like an unsightly red pimple on the soft, white back of some sultry and voluptuous woman.
— FROM *Population 12,360*

Roberta Shagland parked her Volkswagen on Genesee Street, the town's main thoroughfare. She parked in front of The Book Mart. Beside her on the seat was a cellophane-wrapped novel from the Mart's lending library. It was this book which had come like a sudden avalanche on Cayuta, New York, leaving its populace shaken and angry; this book which had put Cayutians under some merciless microscope, like a community of wiggling amoebas, swimming in stagnancy. It was the woman who wrote this book whom Roberta Shagland hated, and her name was Gloria Wealdon.

Miss Shagland picked the book up and rubbed her fingers along the cellophane, along the author's name, as though with that motion she could rub out the name. GLOR-I-A first — *rubbed out* — then Wealdon. Next, the title: *POPULATION 12,360*.... That would leave just the blurb above the title: "... a searing novel of a small town by a daring new writer." She ran her thumb across those words, then dropped the book in her tote bag on the Volkswagen's floor. For a moment, she sat behind the wheel watching the people pass back and forth on Genesee.... How many of them were hurt by Gloria Wealdon's novel; how many angry, amused, disgusted? As much as she wanted to ponder this, she found she was able only to think of Milo Wealdon, Gloria's husband — big, good-looking, strong, gentle Milo — and of the way he had been maligned in the book.

Miss Shagland had arrived in Cayuta in the middle of January, five months ago. She had come to fill the post left vacant by the sudden demise of Cayuta High's dietician. A farm-born, awkward and shy woman nearing the end of her twenties, she had come from a horribly confused settlement on the outskirts of ever-expanding Syracuse, New York. It was a settlement that was ugly and treeless and smelly, with the noise and odor and look of growing industry. She had hated the greasy diners near there, the half-dozen used car lots, the junkyard, the smoke, and the new, new — everything about them new — ranch house developments that were all alike — little lawns, hugging the highway, pink or bright blue or lemon yellow, within walking distance of the shopping center with its sleek A&P, drugstore, Five & Ten. Modern and young and obvious and vulgar.

She had come from there to Cayuta in dead winter, so that it did not look as fabulous and amazing as it did now in May, but she had known what Cayuta would look like. In her imagination she had undressed those great hills of their snow like an eager lover in his erotic fantasies; and she had with dreamer's kisses put the blush of color to all the trees and brush surrounding. She had known that Cayuta would be like so many of the lakeside cities in the Finger Lakes, hiding behind and between huge green mounds. A sudden surprise of glinting blue water, church spires, farm houses dotting the approach; then the city limits sign, the tall Victorian houses with their peaked gables making the new ones in between seem squat and crazy-modern; the immense Norway maples and horse chestnuts ticking the green soft long lawns; and the sprinklers now, turned on at summer's near-beginning, and at the lake the boats being scraped and painted, their sails airing; all of it — Cayuta.

How had Milo Wealdon put it?

"Cayuta," he had said, "is like a perennial plant. Some

plants — the annuals and the biennials — are pretty for a while, but they change and die. Towns are like that too. Cayuta's not. It's like a perennial — it stays. It dies down in the winter, but renews its growth again in the spring."

Milo Wealdon was the physical education teacher at Cayuta High where Roberta Shagland was dietician. Even though she knew him very, very slightly, Miss Shagland knew he was different from any man she had ever met. When he spoke (just those few times, just those precious few times) it was like a poet speaking; still, her nose came just to the level of the huge muscle on his arm, and she had seen him once outside the gym, near the lockers, in shorts, and she had trembled to notice his build; and she had thought about how much a man he looked…. She had thought about that quite a lot.

As if to force the subject from her mind that morning, Roberta Shagland jerked up the Volkswagen's door handle and got out. The suddenness of her movement caused her to hit her head, and her own "Damn!" made her feel naughty and slightly sophisticated, but she was neither of these. She slipped a dime into the parking meter and walked toward The Book Mart; and she did not even have to look closely at the window to know that there was only one book on display. Twenty-five, thirty, fifty — how many copies of that one book arranged every which way?

She nearly collided with an elderly woman standing near the entrance. A parent. She recognized old Mrs. Waterhouse from out on Grove Street, who still came to P.T.A. meetings though all her children were well into their thirties and had children of their own.

They said hello, but Mrs. Waterhouse had something to add, and Roberta Shagland turned to listen. "I beg your pardon?" she said. "I didn't hear you."

"I said if Miss Dare was still with the Mart a thing like

this would never have happened."

"You mean the window display."

"Miss Dare had taste."

"I never knew her," said Miss Shagland.

"She was a fine girl. She wouldn't have kept that woman's book in stock!"

Roberta Shagland had often heard Gloria Wealdon described as "That Woman" since the novel's publication. "That Woman," Cayutians said, as though her name was a strange one to their ears; as though her name were not worth remembering — the way an irate wife might refer to her husband's mistress, or the local chapter of the Women's Temperance Union might identify a female barfly. Gloria Wealdon's name was as well known to Cayutians as cod to Boston, steel to Pittsburgh. It was not a strange name to many outside Cayuta either. People "out of touch" might not have heard the name — pedants, coal miners, expatriates who had suddenly returned from abroad and who wanted to know if she was a murderess, a television star or what? — but most everyone else in the country knew that Gloria Wealdon was synonymous with sex and money, that she had written a novel which the *Times* had called "a feverishly inept exposé of a festering small town," and that it was selling like knishes in the Catskills.

"I don't know why anyone would waste their time on such trash," said old Mrs. Waterhouse.

Roberta Shagland's tote bag felt suddenly enormously heavy. "Yes," she murmured. "It mustn't be a very worthwhile book."

"When Miss Dare ran The Book Mart, she sold literature. Now look." Mrs. Waterhouse waved her hand at the display. "Trash!"

"Goodbye, Mrs. Waterhouse," said Roberta Shagland.

Mrs. Waterhouse nodded, still standing before the window, shaking her head and mumbling angrily.

Inside the Mart, the clerk beamed at Miss Shagland when he saw her take the book from her bag.

"We've been waiting for this!" he said. "We have a waiting list as long as Genesee Street!"

"I'm sorry if I kept people waiting."

She was not sorry at all. She felt sorry for Milo Wealdon, and if she had kept other Cayutians from reading his wife's descriptions of him, she was glad.

The clerk said, "We just got a whole new order of the book in, but you know how people are. People don't want to buy anything they can borrow for a few cents a day."

"Yes," Roberta Shagland said.

"I'm not casting any aspersions on you, Miss Shagland. Don't get me wrong. On a schoolteacher's pay, I don't blame you if you don't buy books."

"I buy books. Some books."

"I always put my foot in my mouth. I didn't mean anything like that."

"I just wouldn't buy this book."

"It's pretty exciting though, isn't it? I mean, someone from right here in Cayuta writing — " but when he saw that Roberta Shagland was not indicating any enthusiasm, he did not bother to finish the sentence.

He took a piece of paper and began to figure.

When he was finished, he looked embarrassed.

"You've had this out for some time, Miss Shagland."

"I know."

"It seems a shame."

"Well, how much do I owe you?"

"You had it for ninety-three days, Miss."

"And that comes to?"

"It comes to $2.79, Miss," said the clerk. "I mean, you *could* have bought it, just about."

When Roberta Shagland handed him the three dollars, her hands were trembling. The hiccups came while she was waiting for her change. Unable to bear it, she left the Mart.

"What's the matter with her?" the clerk said. "She wasn't even in the book!"

A man buying greeting cards said, "Maybe that's what's the matter with her."

Two

"What's the matter with Miles?"
"Listen," she said. "I don't love him. I can't stand him. And the frosting on the cake is that he's lousy in bed!"
— FROM *Population 12,360*

Milo Wealdon stood by the kitchen sink in the small, sky-blue, split-level house on Alden Avenue. He watched his wife hurry along the well-worn shortcut through the fields behind their house. She was on her way to their neighbors, the Fultons. For a coffee klatsch with Fern, she'd said. He had mumbled something about the fact two people couldn't have a klatsch; a klatsch meant three people or more.

"Jealous because you weren't asked along?" she'd said.

"Don't be ridiculous," he'd said, "I'm just telling you what a klatsch is. Look it up in the dictionary."

Gloria had laughed. "You look it up. I'm in a rush."

He couldn't find it in the dictionary. He had been so eager to prove to himself that he was right, that he had run for the Webster's while Gloria was putting her coat on. Now while he watched her go along the path behind their house, he was angry with himself for having tried to find out the definition for klatsch. What did it matter? Why, again, had he been goaded into pettiness?

He continued to watch her until she was out of sight.

She had her hair done up in socks — his old ones — and she wore one of his freshly-laundered white shirts, though he had asked her *please,* if she had to wear his shirts, to wear one of the colored ones. The pants were her own, old black frontier pants, which were rapidly being disowned by her hips, thighs and buttocks. As sloppy as she was, Gloria did not like gaining weight. She counted her calories now; she only had 1,000 calories a day that *she* knew about. Milo's lips tipped in a grin as he recalled fixing her coffee that morning. He had not used saccharin the way she'd thought. He had used two teaspoons of sugar.

On her feet, Gloria wore those ugly boats — her space shoes, which she had discovered in New York City. They looked grotesque to Milo; prehistoric. His dentist wore them too. Until Gloria had come home with a pair, Dr. Saperstein was the only person in Cayuta, New York, to own them. Milo could not forget that the first time he had ever seen them on Saperstein he had thought that they made good sense.

Your feet needed room. Your feet could get like houseplants that are cooped up in containers that don't give the roots room to grow in. Such plants become pot-bound. Milo had had some Rosary Peas die on him, because he hadn't given the roots room. He had felt as bad about that as another man might feel about starving a dog.... After Saperstein showed Milo his shoes, Milo had written down the address of a place where they were sold in Syracuse, New York. He had kept it in his wallet for months, before he had decided they were too expensive. When Gloria had unpacked her pair, Milo had explained in a contemptuous way that she had been taken in again; he had said you'll believe *anything,* won't you, Glo! Any old thing anyone comes along and tells you. *Space* shoes, migod!

His mood that Saturday morning in mid-May was striped with rancor on the one hand, clemency on the other. Since her sudden success as a novelist, Gloria seemed to take even more pride than usual in her unkempt appearance. What was the sense in being a success if you were going to look like something the cat dragged home? That was something he couldn't figure out. He thought somehow Gloria would return from her publicity trip with a whole new wardrobe. He expected black silk dresses, cuckoo hats with dippy feathers on them, jewelry, maybe even a fur. He should have known better. For her photograph on the book jacket, Gloria had worn the same outfit she was wearing this morning; and when he had picked up *The Cayuta Citizen* one evening three weeks ago, Glo's picture had confronted him on page three. It was a U.P. news photo of her press conference in a suite at the Waldorf. She was wearing a mannish trench coat, over a pair of Milo's old blue-and-white-striped Orion pajamas. Underneath the photograph there was a caption:

The uninhibited authoress of Population 12,360 says she wrote her book for laughs. But reports from her home town indicate few people think it's funny!

Milo's fury was always arrested by certain scenes that flashed across the screen of his memory; the pitiful incidents of the past, which belied the present. He remembered how he used to fold Glo in his arms and rock her like a small child, to reassure her after she returned from an afternoon of bridge at Fern Fulton's — usually with one of her stomach aches which overtook her whenever she felt inferior.

"I'm just not like them, Milo," she would sob.

"Pay them no attention, honey."

"My clothes are all wrong, my hair, everything!"

"I like the way you — "

"I wear the same things they do, but I look — washed-out, colorless, plain!"

"Do you want to know something, Glo?" Milo would say. "When I was staking out our grounds here, I chose those hornbeam hedges because the tulips would be lost without them. The tulips need something substantial to back them up. Do you understand what I'm saying, Glo? Season after season I've seen the flowers come and go, but the plain old ordinary hedge stays. You can count on it; and the hedge doesn't need the tulips, remember that. The tulips need the hedge for contrast, but the hedge doesn't need — "

"Oh, for the love of Christ, shut up, Milo!"

"If you'd listen, you'd see that — "

"That I was nothing but a plain old ordinary hedge, Milo?"

It was the only way he knew how to philosophize — by talking in terms of the things in life he loved. His gardening; his collection of saints, which he sculptured out of Ivory soap and preserved with Krylon spray enamel; and sometimes, too, the world of sport, though he thought of that more as his vocation than his avocation.

He had become interested in gardening after his marriage to Gloria, but the saints had fascinated him ever since he was in the navy. A shipmate of his, Dacky Kent, a robust, intelligent comedian with aspirations for the priesthood, had entertained him through many long and perilous voyages, telling him stories about famous and infamous saints. Milo used to appreciate particularly Dacky's ability to see the humor in many of the saints' lives; in fact, the first soap sculpture Milo had ever done had been that of Saint Elizabeth of Hungary. Dacky had told him about her during that ironic trip to the Aleutians, when the ship was carrying rations for the troops and the food served on board was stomach-crying skimpy. Through long watches when both of them yearned to break into the hold and devour the precious cargo, Dacky told how St. Elizabeth gave so bountifully to the poor that she starved her own household. One day her husband met her going out with her apron filled with something heavy, and he demanded to know what she was carrying. She had told him she was merely taking flowers to the poor — and God had converted the loaves of bread in her apron into flowers, to save the lie. Milo whittled out a meticulous likeness of the saint as he saw her, before the miracle. Dacky raved at his craftsmanship, and howled when he saw the tiny soap loaves in the saint's apron. Before they reached the Aleutians, Dacky made tiny, intricate paper roses, so that one evening when Milo opened his locker he found his Elizabeth carrying flowers in her apron.

After that, Milo made other soap sculptures, all saints. Dacky made a bet with him that before Milo could whittle out the thirty-seven saints of diseases and ills, the eighty-three saints of cities, nations and places, and the ninety-three specialist saints for tradesmen, children, wives, idiots and children, Dacky would be back in mufti, wearing his collar backward. When Dacky was killed years later in an automobile accident, he was in his second year of study for the priesthood. Milo had just finished sculpturing Saint Blaise, saint of sore throats, number thirty-two of diseases and ills.... Now, Milo was all the way to the brewers' saint, Florian. He had one hundred thirty-one sculptures, and he knew quite a lot about sainthood.

At first, during their marriage, Gloria had seemed to enjoy the stories of the saints. During their courtship, too, she had given the promise of sharing Milo's hobby with him. Gloria had always been a very insecure person, and in the beginning, when they met on the Cornell campus and began going to The Ivy for beers, they had seemed an unlikely couple, even to themselves. In those days, Milo was *it*. Track star, football hero, DKE, big, smiling, hand-some — he was a catch. Gloria had never made a sorority. She pretended she had chosen to be an Independent; pretended to scorn the close-knit little coterie of Kappas, Pi Phi's, or Tri Delts, but Milo had been told by his fraternity brothers that she had gone through rush week and hadn't made it. Milo's fraternity brothers were always criticizing her: her looks (she was very skinny in those days, and as sloppy as ever); her rowdy "hail-fellow-well-met" personality, which soured whatever remaining semblance of femininity she had; and her almost defiant, angry mood switches, which led her to pound you heartily on the back in one turn and snarl sullenly at you in the other.

Milo himself was slightly amazed at his own persistence in dating Glo. He would tell himself that he was simply going to ask her to see a movie with him "sometime next week" (maybe because he felt she needed him: he could do *that* much, couldn't he?) and then he would find himself actually cajoling her to be his date for the DKE hop. He, Milo Wealdon, one of the most popular men on campus, begging *her* to let him take her out! He had read once something that H. L. Mencken had written, something about winking at a homely girl if you wanted to remember him. Was it Mencken's epitaph? Whatever it was, Milo remembered that much, and when he first saw Gloria, he was compelled to pay special attention to her. She was standing off to one side, in a crowd at Willard Straight Hall. She seemed little and left over, and terribly nervous and embarrassed, and Milo had gone over to her and begun asking her questions, telling her anecdotes, making a fuss over her. Why?

And why, after that, had he kept on calling her, waiting outside classrooms for her, *imploring* her (yes, that was what it had been) to see him? She seemed no more flattered by his attentions than the most beautiful, popular, sought-after campus queen, and probably, Milo realized, a lot less. Over and over she complained to him about her inadequacies, and yet the fact that he said repeatedly that he liked her and everything about her never seemed to make her feel better. In a very subtle way his reassurances seemed only to make him appear all the more a fool in her eyes. As though she were saying: Well, all right, I know I'm no bargain, and if you're too dumb to see that, then you're no bargain either.

In a way, sandwiched between their gradual getting used to one another, between the rare moments when they would laugh together, say casual endearments, and eventually neck in the back seat of Milo's old Plymouth, there was an uncanny unfitness about them as a couple. Even physically. Their noses were always colliding in an embrace; she would laugh just as Milo was about to kiss her, and his lips would be bruised by her teeth. They were clumsy on the dance floor, though with anyone else Milo was an excellent dancer. Even alone, when they had conversation, the normal rhythm was lacking: they interrupted each other; they both paused at the same time, so that there were long silences when neither of them could think of what to say, and when thoughts did occur to them, they came simultaneously and resulted in a near-shouting head-on collision. There were other things, too. Milo felt sorry for people Gloria felt were just stupid. Milo would say, "If someone would just give him a chance," while Gloria would say, "He's obnoxious, he deserves to be ignored." Milo was a liberal. He believed in racial equality, and sometimes things he read in the newspaper would make him very angry; things about a race riot, or an example of discrimination — things like that. Whenever he talked about it, Gloria would lash out at him for being in a fraternity Jews couldn't join; she would call him a hypocrite, and a bigot, and the discussion would end with her malicious and triumphant attack on him, with the

issue he had brought up forgotten. Gloria was anti-reli-
gion, anti-Republican, anti-management, anti-everything,
until Milo found himself more and more reluctant to talk
about such matters with her. More and more he kept
silent, simply listening, except when Gloria told him about
the unfair things that had happened to her — the snubs,
the ridicule, all the offenses against her, which were imagined in some cases, in others real. Then Milo would speak
gently, compassionately. "You're just as pretty as other
girls, Glo. You just have it in your mind you're not." (A
lie.) "You did have a rough childhood, and you *did* come
from pretty poor circumstances, but you had the guts to
rise above it, didn't you? And that's something." (The
truth.) "You are well-liked, Glo. People like you.... I do
need you, honey. Don't say I don't need you." And so it
went, falsehoods, truths, words pouring out of him to
make her feel better — his arms locking out all the injuries,
his mouth kissing away her anxieties. Why?

For a while, in the back seat of the Plymouth, Milo
never tried to do more than kiss Glo. She was not particularly passionate, but she seemed to enjoy it when he
was. As he experimented more and more, he realized this.
He kissed her tenderly and slowly; then roughly, with a
bare edge of violence in his manner.
He kissed her eyes and her ears and her neck, and he let
his tongue slip into her mouth. When there were no more
ways left to kiss her, he began to tell her how attractive
the rest of her was. She denied this, and he became all the
more vehement in his protests. For a period, he seemed to
dwell constantly on her lovely bosom, thinking of everything on earth he could compare it with, as he pressed her
close to him. It seemed to anger her, until he felt he must
prove that he meant it by fondling her. The only reason
he had never tried before was that he was slightly old-
fashioned. He did not think it was fair to a girl. He did

not like men who took advantage of women.

Tortured by a suspicion that Gloria would never believe his well-meant compliments about her breasts until he paid her the supreme compliment of going up under her sweater in a moment of passion, Milo abandoned his moral concepts. What happened then completely shocked him. Before he knew what had happened, two pieces of foam rubber whipped him in the eye.

"Here!" she screamed at him. "That's all you want anyway! Now for God's sake, leave me alone!"

He was left sitting in the old Plymouth by himself, with a pair of falsies on his lap.

It was that incident which had inspired Milo's first gift to Gloria — his sculpture of Saint Lucy. He wrote a little note to accompany the present:

> *This is Lucy. She's the patron saint for those afflicted in the eyes. She's supposed to have lived in Syracuse, and to have suffered martyrdom there about 303. There was a nobleman who wanted to marry her. She was supposed to be very beautiful; her eyes particularly were beautiful. The nobleman kept telling her so, until one day she tore out her eyes saying: "Now let me live to God." Her day is December 13th. Will you marry me, or am I stuck with the falsies the way the nobleman was stuck with Lucy's eyes?*

His proposal was accepted.

Gloria still kept Saint Lucy under a small glass globe on the bureau in their bedroom.

After their marriage, Gloria had genuinely tried to change. She had a permanent wave, and she took care buying clothes. Whenever they entertained, she fixed new dishes and fussed throughout the evening, hurrying to empty ashtrays, refresh drinks, put pillows behind the guests' backs, trying to say and do the right thing and look the right way. It was overdone — the permanent, the clothes, the hostessing — all of it. They lived in the town Milo was raised in, so that Glo was a newcomer. Milo had never thought of Cayuta as being an unfriendly community, but it soon seemed that way — from Gloria's vantage point. His friends were as disinclined to accept her as his fraternity brothers had been. Her failure to win their acceptance hurt him deeply. At the same time, he wished Glo could just relax, just not try so damnably hard to be liked.

He got his wish. Eventually she stopped trying altogether. She went out of her way to dress like some kind of hoyden years younger than herself. She wore blue jeans and flannel shirts (hanging outside her pants) and she cut her hair and combed it in some crazy way that made her look as though she had been caught in a wind tunnel. No make-up. No embellishments of any kind. She was just there; take her or leave her. Milo sensed what she was trying to tell Cayuta: *I could be attractive if I wanted to be, but I couldn't care less — not about any of you!* It was along about this same time that she began aspiring to the arts: first oil paints, until she tired of cleaning out the brushes, only to start again at her miserable, glaringly-poor efforts; then the guitar (her fingers weren't long enough, she complained — you have to have very long fingers); and, ultimately, writing.

She had worked hard on that novel. No one knew that better than Milo. She had sat at that typewriter like someone driven, day after day, and sometimes far into the early morning.

"I'll show them," she would say.

"Show them what, Glo?"

He needn't have asked. He had seen Fern Fulton's condescending smiles directed at Glo at parties, seen them and resented them, and yet, how many times had he himself flinched inwardly when Glo said something like "Oh, sperry-grass, with that old Dutch sauce Holland days," at a dinner when asparagus was served, or "Where's the wash rag and soap," when a finger bowl was placed before her. And could he ever forget that afternoon at the Cayuta Country Club when Min Stewart had bent over to retrieve a glove she had dropped and Gloria had goosed her? Min Stewart, Cayuta's formidable septuagenarian social lioness.... It was no mystery to anyone why Min had kept Glo out of the Cayuta Ladies Birthday Club. There was not a soul in Cayuta who believed Min's excuse that there were already too many members in the club whose birthdays were in January. Perhaps Glo's major forte was her devastating ability to choose the most inappropriate, unpardonable thing to do or say at a social gathering. Milo still blushed to recall the chicken-in-the-pot supper at Second Presbyterian church, when Glo had excused herself during the soup course with the announcement: "When you gotta go, you gotta go." She had followed that vulgarity by glancing across the table at Jay Mannerheim, Cayuta's new psychoanalyst, and saying, "I suppose my toilet training was lousy!"

"I'll show them I'm somebody," Glo had vowed. "I'll write a book that'll make their ears burn!"

While Gloria pounded the typewriter, Milo did another sculpture. It was of Saint Agatha, patron saint of the arts, and Milo took exceptional care with this one. He hoped it would be placed at the other end of their bureau in the bedroom, opposite Saint Lucy. When he presented it to Glo, she said, "You'd like me to be a martyr, wouldn't you, Milo? You'd like it if I was an old piece of soap that you could coat with plastic and put on the shelf beside the other ones? Saint Agatha, huh?" she had snickered, and then snapped the sculpture in half, leaving it there on the cardtable where she worked, beside the ashtray of cigarette butts and the wads and wads of wrinkled typing paper.

That was the night Milo got that splitting headache, the first one he had ever had in his life. It was the same night he had accidentally spilled the scalding tea on Glo, after he had prepared it to dissolve the aspirins faster and tripped carrying it across to his chair.

He supposed, too, it was the night he had first thought of his plot for revenge. Those headaches came more and more frequently after that, and each time the plot thickened. It was the only relief for the pain....

Glancing down at the dirty breakfast dishes stacked in the sink that morning, Milo Wealdon sighed.

He raised his fingers to his lips, and sucked in smoke from his near-spent morning cigarette. Revenge was a strange word for a man like Milo to have in his vocabulary. It was as unlikely as "hate," or "greed," or "lust," or "evil." Words like that had always been meaningless to him, applicable only to situations he was unconnected with. Yet today, the word revenge loomed larger than any other. Today was the day, wasn't it? Again, he sighed.

At thirty-six he was in excellent form. His long body was strong and hard and agile. He was proud of the fact that he looked the way an instructor in Physical Education ought to look and usually didn't. It was perhaps the only conceit he had left, his physique, and it played no small part in his revenge. At one time he had entertained the thought that his curly brown hair, his pug nose, and his round brown eyes lent his countenance the same youthful handsomeness his body exhibited, but Gloria had called a halt on that fantasy. In her novel she had described him as *A Hercules from the neck down, and a runny-nosed bull dog from the neck up, with eyes as lusterless as the eyes of a fish on the end of a hook.*

There was an expression of tired irritation on Milo's face, suddenly aggravated by the fact that he realized he was running his tongue along the inside of his lower lip, the same way the stupid, weak-willed main character in Gloria's novel always did whenever *he* was angry; the same way Milo always did too, though he had not been aware of it until *Population 12,360* was published. Now, he supposed, more than a million other people were aware of it as well. It had not helped matters any that Glo had named the numbskull hero Miles, or that she had dedicated her novel:

TO MY HUSBAND, MILO: A JUST REWARD

As the phone rang, and Milo went to answer it, he displaced his anger and indignation at what Gloria had done to him by deciding for the umpteenth time that whether or not *he* deserved to have *his* seams split open with a razor so that the sawdust all came spilling out, certainly the rest of the people in Cayuta, New York, did not deserve it! Glo had chosen a particularly vitriolic way of "showing" them; one that made her all the more a maverick in everyone's eyes.

When he lifted the phone from its cradle, he spent the last of his rancor by barking his greeting.

There was a pause. Then Milo recognized Stanley Secora's voice.

"Gee, Mr. Wealdon, I'm sorry to bother you. I — I just wondered if it would be okay for me to drop by this afternoon. I mean, if *Mrs.* Wealdon is going to be home."

Immediately Milo felt obliged to sound enormously pleased that Stanley had called. It was partly because the timid and shy invariably reacted on him in such a way that he found himself duty-bound to make them feel wanted. But also, Milo felt this way toward Stanley because he knew the boy had developed an immense crush on Gloria, with the resulting error that Stanley believed he was destined to be a writer himself.

Vaguely, Glo was aware of him. Summers, Stanley cut the lawn sometimes, or helped put up the storm windows in the late fall. At odd intervals, he had helped Milo build compost piles for the lawn, plant Japanese quince along the side yard, and paint the garage. Except for seeing him those times, and hearing from Milo of Stanley's pathetic efforts in his Thursday evening tumbling class, Gloria had little reason at all to be aware of Stanley until her book was published.

Then, suddenly, Stanley began to talk of nothing else, of no one else. "Mrs. Wealdon" became his idol. He began to try to extract all sorts of miscellaneous information about her from Milo. He wondered about everything, from her preference in sweets to how many hours sleep a night she needed.

Once, during the tumbling class, Milo had snapped at him: "She likes coconut ice and she sleeps seven hours a night, Secora, but what the devil has any of that got to do with *you!*"

After that, Stanley stopped coming to Milo's class. He called once to announce that he was writing a novel, and would like "Mrs. Wealdon" to read it when she returned from New York. Milo felt so sorry he had lost his temper with the boy that he very graciously suggested Stanley write her, assuring him Glo would be tremendously interested in his work.

By telephone, Milo persuaded Gloria to drop Secora a post card, telling him to call her after the 20th of May, when she would be back in Cayuta.

It was now the 27th of May. Stanley had called eight times.

Milo said, "I'm delighted that you called. You know, we miss you at tumbling class."

There had never been anyone more inept at the sport or more ill-suited to it than the dumpy, bespectacled stock clerk. Yet, in the beginning, Milo had never had a more eager pupil. He could not but admire Secora's spirit. It wanted to soar, but it was weighed down; it was like a lily whose underground suckers imprisoned it.

Stanley said, "I'm working most of the time on my novel, Mr. Wealdon. Mrs. Wealdon sure inspired me. I mean, if *she* can write one of these best sellers, than I guess — " He paused; then he began to stutter. "I — I d-d-didn't mean it th-th-that way, Mr. Wealdon, I m-meant — "

Milo said, "I know what you meant, fellow."

"I meant she's an inspiration."

"Yes," Milo said, "I know."

He glanced down at the telephone pad on the table. The date was circled on Gloria's engagement calendar. Written across the page in large, triumphant letters, were three words:

PITTS ARRIVES TONIGHT.

Milo had not yet met Gloria's literary agent, but already he hated him. Hate, another once-remote word that was now close, suffocatingly close.

"I told Mrs. Wealdon Saturdays were my day off," Stanley continued, "and she said I should drop by this afternoon. You have the track meet and all, so I wouldn't be horning in on your time, would I, Mr. Wealdon?"

Horning in on *his* time. Milo wanted to laugh, but he couldn't — not any more.

In smaller scribbling mid-way down the same page on the calendar Milo read: *Lunch with Min Stewart! Hotel. 12:30.*

He ran his finger across the words, and put his thumb down hard on the exclamation point, as though squashing a bug.

He said, "If I were you, Stanley, I'd drop by a little earlier. Before noon. Mrs. Wealdon isn't here now, but I know she'll be back in time to change her clothes."

If Secora were to show up before she could get downtown for her luncheon date with Min Stewart, Glo would have to give him a little time.

"You sure it's all right, Mr. Wealdon? I don't want to horn in on you, and I know she said her agent was coming from New York City later today."

"You won't be horning in, Stanley. And her agent won't be here until tonight."

Again, Milo felt the fury pulse through him. It was Pitts this and Pitts that and Pitts hung the moon, ever since Gloria had met her agent.

He said, "Come over about eleven-forty-five, Stanley."

"Thanks, Mr. Wealdon," Secora said; and then he said, "Oh, and Mr. Wealdon … you're doing all right too, aren't you?"

"What do you mean?" Milo's voice was taut, defensive. For the craziest moment he found himself thinking of the new dietician at the high school, Miss Shagland. His ears flushed scarlet, and he felt the same inner punch to his emotions he might have felt had he been caught with Roberta Shagland *in flagrante delicto.*

"I mean about the team winning Wednesday," Secora said uncertainly. "I mean, that was great coaching, Mr. Wealdon. *That's* hard work too."

After Milo hung up, he felt absurd. Roberta Shagland hardly knew he existed, he decided. But that wasn't true either. For four days in a row he had carried her tray in the high school cafeteria, hadn't he?

She giggled a lot, too, at things he said. Still, that was no sign she even thought about him; not long thoughts. She was too shy. She had those enormous ankles. Rudy Unger, the science teacher, called her "piano legs." The first time Milo heard him say it, he felt like knocking him down and kicking in his teeth.

What control did a woman have over her ankles.

Milo was sick and tired of his own mind. It was as though he were caught up in Gloria's winds, being propelled by them down some strange bright streets upon which he was destined to become the silly soul he had lately seemed more and more on the verge of being. Nights, he had those nightmares of being caught naked in the lobby of the Cayuta Hotel — nights when he could sleep at all, that is. And during the day? His headaches, and the plan — the plan for revenge.

Why couldn't he just let it be, let Glo go on having her affair with this Pitts? What did it matter to him? What did Miss Shagland matter to him, for that matter? She wanted no part of him. Did anything matter to him …?

He thought of his geraniums, of the way the leaves were curling from the inside. That meant cyclamen mites. He would have to use a good nicotine spray on them, with some Blackleaf in it. Last year the cyclamen mites had eaten away at his chrysanthemums; he was not going to let them get the geraniums.

Milo sighed again, and it was as though anything and everything he did was a reminder of the book on the bestseller list. For "Miles" was always sighing too: "… endlessly sighing away his existence, in hallways by coat racks, on gravel driveways near garages, in anterooms and elevators, down all the dreary gray-skyed streets, sighing, sighing, sighing."

Glancing down again at the table where the telephone rested, Milo saw Gloria's clipboard under her calendar. Attached to it were the yellow scratch sheets on which she wrote her notes. He took up the clipboard and began to read:

NOTES FOR A NEW NOVEL ABOUT A WOMAN WHOSE BOOK HITS THE BEST SELLER LIST

Tell story just way happened to me. Never wrote novel before. Decided to expose town. What happens when return to Cayuta.

1. Fern Fulton's awe of me, despite she in book. Her failure to mention how she felt about herself in book. Afraid of next book I write?

2. Clucks like Secora who want me to read their stuff.

3. Minnie Stewart asking me for lunch despite fact I had plenty in book about Louie. What want? Apologize to me for past behave?

4. Milo's dumbfounded awe of me even though made ass of him. He jealous.

Under "four" there was a list:

ripe olives
wine (what kind Pitts like? Ravel? Clavel?)
tissue paper
stamps
corn holders
cake knife
a-acid pills

Milo Wealdon tossed the clipboard back on the telephone table.

He ran his tongue along the inside of his lower lip. Then he felt the sudden slight beating near his temples, saw before him the bright, pulsating zigzag line. It was the fuzzy warning of another migraine on its way.

Three

"It's not therapy," Fernanda said.
"Then what is it?"
"Just because he's my analyst, you think it's ther-
apy!"
"Then what is it?"
"Good Lord, it's an affair. We're having an af-
fair!"
And that was like Fernanda too, not to see any-
thing peculiar about the fact she and her psycho-
analyst were lovers.
       — FROM *Population 12,360*

Fern Fulton said, "Honestly Glo, you've got the whole town right on its ear!"

They were sipping Nescafé in the Fultons' dinette, just off the kitchen.

Gloria Wealdon no longer thought Fern looked like Ida Lupino. It used to be that no matter how Fern was dressed, no matter how tired or hungover Fern was, Gloria saw her through the spectacles of awe, glad and beholden to be her friend, convinced that Freddy Fulton's wife was fabulous and exciting and tragically wasted on Cayuta. Part of it, Gloria supposed, was due to the fact Fern wasn't a native of the small upstate New York town; she was a native New Yorker. Her father, William B. Everight, had been very rich once. Gloria remembered a time, during the early years of their friendship, when Fern told her:

"Dad had a seat on the exchange, you know."

"Oh?" Gloria answered, wondering what that meant, wondering why she should be so impressed.

She knew she should be by the way Fern had said it.

"We began liquidating in 1930. Dad sold the seat then.

We really needed the money."

"I didn't know you were ever that poor, Fern."

"Well, we weren't really *poor.*"

"We always were. Really poor. But even we never had to sell furniture."

Gloria never forgot how Fern had laughed then. They were all sitting in the Fultons' cream-colored living room — Freddy, Fern, Gloria and Milo. Even Freddy laughed, and Gloria, immediately aware that she had made another faux pas of some sort, forced laughter too, trying to pretend she had really meant it as a joke. But Milo had intensified the error. His ears were that red color. His tone of voice wallowed in protest at the Fultons' unfairness. He was Christ on the cross again, martyr for the innocent and ignorant.

"Now just a minute," he said, "just a minute. You can't expect Glo to know anything about the New York Stock Exchange." He turned to her, placatingly, his light blue eyes sorry for her again. "It's not a real chair, Glo. A seat on the exchange is actually a position; it's a profession. It's worth thousands and thousands."

Fern stopped laughing long enough to say, "Four hundred and sixty thousand dollars."

There were so many times like that time.

Once, Fern had confided to Gloria that before she met Freddy her father used to have a "Proudfoot" done on any young man who dated her more than six times. She had laughed: "And look who I ended up marrying, the head of a pharmaceutical house in Cayuta, New York!"

"What's a 'Proudfoot'?" Gloria had asked.

"It's a service that finds out exactly what a man is worth. A rich man. They wouldn't even bother with someone like Freddy."

Gloria had tried to commit the word to memory, to save it and use it sometime in the future. When the time came, during another of the Fultons' dinner parties, Gloria had used it wrongly. Fleetfoot, she had said. More laughter, with Milo saving face for her again. "Look now," he had said, "we're just poor relations of you folks. You can't expect the ordinary field daisy to know anything about the bouvardias."

Field daisy, he had said; but bouvardias ... not field dai*sies* and bouvardias.

Driving home that night Gloria said, "And I suppose *you* knew it was Proudfoot and not Fleetfoot."

"You try too hard," he said. "You remind me of Timmy Boulton."

"Is he a saint or a shrub?"

"He's Ken Boulton's teen-ager. He's great at hockey, superb at tennis, and the best swimmer we have at Cayuta High. But his ambition is to be a basketball star. He's five-foot-one."

"You have to stick your neck out if you want to get anywhere, Milo."

"Sure," said Milo, "if you're a turtle."

In the garage, after he turned off the ignition key and the lights, he had tried to kiss her.

"Glo, you're crying!"

"You mean you can see me from all the way up there, Milo?"

"What do you mean, from all the way up there?"

"From your heights."

"Wait a minute, Glo. Just a minute."

"I don't want to sit in the garage philosophizing at midnight, Milo. You better put the hoe back up against the wall, or you'll run over it in the morning."

"We're going to leave everything at this point?"

"Yes, because that's the point it's at. You can't make a silk purse out of a sow's ear, Milo," she'd said, getting out of the car, "or a bouvardia out of a common field daisy."

Somewhere about that time she had stopped being annoyed at Milo's imperturbable calm, stopped exaggerating every unintentional affront of his and stopped enjoying his desperate, guilt-worn attempts to get off the hook once she did exaggerate one. She reached that stage in her loveless marriage where it was no longer satisfying to punish him for having been the only man who would marry her. She passed to an intermediary stage in which her aim became to make his best friends like her better than they liked him.

Milo was extremely popular, so the task she set herself was not easy. She could never accomplish it by tearing him down. Her mode of attack was to do it by playing on his friends' sympathies, by making her own life seem so much more heartbreaking and pathetic than his (which had been about as exciting as a glass of warm water) that everyone would suddenly see them in contrast — Milo, easy-going, puttering, patience-suffering, dull; herself, ingenuous at times (all right!), but impulsive, Bohemian, anxious, sensitive.

She had made several tries in the beginning. There was that hot Fourth of July when they were all at the Cayuta Country Club for the golfing tournament. Somehow, ever since Gloria Wealdon had met Min Stewart, she had thought of her as being absolutely like Ethel Barrymore. Milo used to complain: "How can you keep on saying people are like this movie star and that one? You don't even know what those people in Hollywood are like!" He could never understand that it wasn't the star really, but the composite picture of the star from every role she or he had ever played. A Bette Davis was always nervous and lighting cigarettes and pacing around dark rooms; a Clark Gable was bare-chested, uncombed, laughing and swilling whiskey, and hiding his heart-tearing sincerity. A Rita Hayworth had a past, but she was trying to live it down, if smart-alec men would only let her. And an Ethel

Barrymore? An Ethel Barrymore oozed dignity, poise; dripped with family trees and crystal chandeliers; but underneath, an Ethel Barrymore admired plain, old-fashioned, pull-yourself-up-by-the-boot-straps individuality. That was why Min Stewart reminded Gloria of Ethel Barrymore. Why else would Min have married a war hero who could have had any job he wanted in 1918 and came back to Cayuta to run his drug store, because he liked being a druggist? Min Stewart had a fortune, by Cayuta's standards, and she was a Genesee County Wadsworth, but she married for love, and love was neither rich nor high-born.

So that afternoon in July at the country club, when Min bent down to pick up her glove, Gloria Wealdon gave her fanny a little pinch. It seemed a fun thing to do, a little crazy gesture to make Min laugh and like her. Instead, Min froze, and even Milo could not think of anything to say to come to his wife's defense. It had been a simple impulse; it had become another horrible, horrible mistake.

"Whatever made you do it, Glo?" Milo had asked. "My God, I hope you don't think Ethel Barrymore would have taken it any better?"

"Ethel Barrymore would have laughed," said Gloria Wealdon, knowing full well, finally, that she wouldn't have.

Then there was Gloria's try with Fern Fulton. This time she decided to tell Fern a little about her childhood. She was not going to tell her anything that was not true. She was going to tell her how her mother always tore out the pictures of food in the old magazines neighbors gave them, because Gloria and her brothers were always nearly starving, the family was so poor. She was going to describe how she had found one of the pictures in the wastebasket one day, a picture of angel food cake. She had looked at it, and then she had eaten the paper it was printed on. She was going to tell her that, and countless other incidents like that.

The afternoon she chose to do it was in December. Freddy was at work, as Milo was, and Fern's daughter was in school. They were having coffee and cake in the Fultons' living room and Fern was standing on a ladder, pinning the gold star on top of the Christmas tree. Under the tree there were countless gifts wrapped grandly in silver and green and gold-flecked paper and tied elegantly with expensive ribbons. Everything about the room spelled splendor, extravagance. Fern was dressed in one of her long, lush dressing gowns, with lace peeking out of the sleeves and fine silk snuggled in the lining.

Gloria wore a pair of old blue jeans and a red wool shirt darned at the elbows. Her storm boots were in the hall and she sat in her tired black wool socks that had a hole in the left toe. She had dressed purposely for this moment. No stage seemed better set. At a point when Fern was fixing the star on the evergreen point and complaining about the fact that the caterer for her Saturday evening party had sent her round butter balls instead of butter triangles, Gloria interrupted her.

"It's strange, Fern."

"What darling, that caterer? Well, what do you expect in Cayuta? I should have known better. It isn't that there's anything wrong with round butter balls. I usually prefer them. But last Saturday I wanted — "

"I don't mean about the butter."

"There! The finishing touch! A lovely gold star! What *do* you mean then, honey?"

"I mean, it's strange, for me, anyway, when I look at all this opulence — those gifts and the tree."

"I love Christmas! Even in July I start thinking about what color lights to have. We used green on green last year, with tinsel the only contrast. Do you remember?"

"Yes…. What I mean, though, is the splendor of everything. I guess you've never been without it."

"You call this splendor, honey? I have to laugh sometimes! When I was a kid, and we were living at 420 Park, my father used to buy a tree six times this size. I guess I got my Christmas-bug from him."

"We had many Christmases without any tree," said Glo.

"Oh, I know. Freddy always says, let's not get a big tree. Ginny's all grown up and everything, we don't need a big tree. But I say, listen, that's one thing I insist on, Freddy!"

"We couldn't afford one lots of times."

"Well you have a diller now, don't you, honey? Milo really did a job on those pines in front of your place. If there was a committee in this town that awarded outdoor decoration prizes, why you know who'd win first prize!"

Gloria decided to change her attack, to be direct. "Fern," she said somewhat sharply, "I want to ask you something!"

Fern turned around on the ladder's step. "What?"

"Fern, were you ever *hungry?*"

Fern's face broke into a big smile. "Honey," she said, "I'm starving right this deadly minute. Hand me up some cake, would you, Glo? I want to fix this peppermint stick."

It was always like that with Fern. Gloria got nowhere….

Now as Gloria sat in the dinette with her that morning in May, she noticed for the first time that Fern's ears were pitifully gigantic, that her long face, which had never seemed *that* long, could not bear the burden of the youthful pony-tail style which Fern inflicted on it. Her hair itself was also different somehow. It suffered too obviously the abuse of once-a-week bad rinses, which Fern administered herself rather than go to a beauty parlor and admit it was dyed. Everything about Fern was different in Gloria

Wealdon's eyes.

"Honestly!" Fern said again, and her voice no longer seemed husky and theatrical (it was raucous and "upstate"), "you've got the whole *country* on its ear! Right on its ear, honey! My gawd, I suppose I ought to be serving you coffee in there!" She waved a long, red-nailed hand toward the large dining room around the corner from the dinette.

Gloria could remember when she had no other wish than to live like the Fultons, cushioned in luxurious comfort, wallowing in wall-to-wall, all-wool rugs, warming your brandy with palms cupped around crystal snifters after dinner, talking of trading in last year's Lincoln for the new model.

Now she thought of the simple, elegant modern furniture in her agent's duplex, of the chic parquet floors which Pitts would not let even a scatter rug violate, of the three kinds of wine he invariably served at dinner, and of his small, low-hung Sunbeam Talbot in which they had raced back and forth to Greenwich for "bites to eat" on star-splashed spring nights.

She said, "A lot of people are angry about my book, aren't they?" glancing out of the window to the yard, where Freddy Fulton was fussing with the hedges. Beside him, following him around the way she followed him everywhere — just as Gloria had described it in her novel — was Virginia, the Fultons' ugly teen-age daughter.

"Freddy thinks you've made Ginny's complex worse, that's all," Fern said, toying with her coffee spoon. "I'm sorry he was rude, but he's so damnably over-protective! Glo, you hit the nail right on the head! It's as though we were supposed to do penance or something because Ginny's eyes are slightly crossed."

Slightly! Glo winced. In the novel, Glo had made Ginny lisp instead.

That morning when she had arrived at the Fultons', neither Freddy nor Virginia had spoken.

"And of course," Fern Fulton said, "Freddy imagines himself as something of a Lothario. I suppose his ego was hurt because you showed how uxorious he is. That's a divine word, darling — uxorious! I had to look it up in the dictionary."

Gloria was dying to bring up Pitts' name. She said: "My literary agent said only a woman could write a book in which *all* the wives had such fawning husbands. Pitts is — "

"He should get a look at the husbands around here," Fern cut her off in the customary way. "You can have them, for my money!" Then she looked across at Glo and laughed, crushing her cigarette in the saucer, reaching over and pressing her large hand on Gloria's wrist. "Ah, but *you* don't need anyone's money any more, do you, honey! You're rich and famous and still as cute as a bug! Look at you! Haven't changed a bit! Still running around like a bobby-soxer, wearing Milo's old shirts and — "

This time Gloria interrupted. As she spoke, she had to strain to discipline her eyes from wandering back to stare at Fern's huge ears; at the crushed cigarette, too, put out in the saucer. Had Fern always put out cigarettes there? Had she ever before put one out there?

Gloria said, "Poor Milo. He's the one I feel sorry for."

She knew she should mean it, but she didn't. She remembered Milo's hang-dog look while he was doing the dishes last night, how it had repulsed her. Yet often she suspected she was too hard on him. It was her agent who had made her see that. She remembered one session with Pitts nearly a year ago, when the book was being rewritten. They had been talking about the way her main character (who was Milo, thinly disguised) told fairy tales to his wife when they made love.

Pitts had insisted: "You've got to cut that, Gloria, that

part about the fairy tales."

"Why?"

"In the first place," said Pitts, "you've made him into a shell of a man right through chapter twenty-three. Then suddenly you have him telling these enchanting fairy tales to his wife in bed, all about the great big Prince and the little bitsy Cinderella."

"Enchanting?" Gloria had guffawed at the idea.

"Well, they are, dammit! You expect the readers to believe that a man as colorless as your hero has that much imagination?"

"They were dull stories, Pitts."

"Not by a long shot. They were intriguing! I'm telling you, Gloria, you have to cut them out, or rewrite the book altogether. Cut them out and make him impotent."

Gloria had said, "Milo was never impotent, Pitts."

"I don't care what he was or wasn't. The way this book is now, he's a very dull character up to chapter twenty-three, and then he's suddenly transformed. Don't you see, Gloria? A dull man who makes love by telling stories is no longer dull!"

Gloria couldn't see it.

Pitts had said, "You know, your husband might very well be a much more fascinating person than you think he is. He reminds me of the fellow in the Viceroy ads. You know, the bank clerk who studies marine biology on the side. The man who thinks for himself." Pitts chuckled.

"Milo's a drip."

"Well, I wouldn't call him an average man, from all you've told me. He seems to have many facets to his personality."

"*What* personality?" Gloria had scoffed.

"Okay, have it your way. He's a drip. But have it my way with regard to the novel, agreed? We'll cut the fairy tales. If you want him to be dull and foolish, we've got to."

Gloria agreed to the cut. She said, "I bet you don't tell any stories in bed, Pitts."

Her literary agent had answered: "I can't think of any. That's why I have to make my living selling other people's."

That had been a year ago. Still, though Pitts had made her see, in some vague way, that she had painted Milo too blackly, he could never make her feel differently toward Milo. She could not even feel sorry for him, and she knew the moment she told Fern Fulton that she was sorry for Milo, her own voice belied her.

Fern said, "Milo will hold up all right."

"You and Freddy must have seen a lot of him while I was away."

Fern lit another cigarette. "He was down the day before yesterday helping Freddy prune the hydrangea. He never acts as though anything's bothering him. That's one of the nice things about him."

"Every night he does the dishes," said Gloria, "and every morning; and if he comes home for lunch, every noon! *I* can afford a maid now, whether he can or not. But you know Milo. 'Oh, no,' he says. 'Your money is not going to finance this house. If you won't clean up around here, then I will.' It's hilarious when you think about it. He plays a man by tying an apron around his waist and doing the dishes!"

Fern had nothing to say to that.

There was a pause while both women sucked on their cigarettes. Gloria thought of telling Fern about Pitts then and there, the whole story in delicious detail, but Fern spoke before she could start.

Fern said, "Freddy thinks Milo is unbelievably patient."

"Oh?"

"He said he'd have tossed your belongings into the street long ago. Oh, you know Freddy, Glo — big, old take-the-bull-by-the-horns stuff!"

"What makes him think it's patience?"

"Isn't it?"

"Milo has no spine, that's all. I think he even loves me more, in fact, because I've made an — pardon my French — ass out of him! Doesn't Freddy know Milo by now, Fern?"

Fern shrugged and chuckled. "I told him he'd better *watch out,* because I was making some notes of my own, for a little project of my own. And honey, don't think I couldn't write a book about that man!"

Gloria glanced out the window again, thinking how boring a book about Freddy would be. He was on his knees by the hedges, pulling up weeds. Anything Freddy Fulton *did* know about gardening, Milo had taught him.

In Gloria's novel, she had made the character Miles a stamp collector. That was another of Pitts' changes.

"Make him a collector of plain, ordinary stamps. Not foreign stamps or anything romantic, but plain stamps, the kind you can buy in a package for twenty-five cents at any dime store."

"Milo buys lots of seeds in the dime store. What's the difference?"

"Listen, Gloria," Pitts had said, "I'm not going to try and make you appreciate your husband, at this point. I'm interested in the novel. You're writing about a stupid fellow, but that stuff your character Miles says about plant life, for instance, in the twenty-sixth chapter, is too damn clever."

"For someone who's as sophisticated as you are," Gloria had laughed, "you certainly come up with peculiar ideas about what's clever in this life."

"You just take my word about books," said Pitts, "never mind life."

Gloria had told him she'd take his word about both; and anything else he could come up with.

As Gloria looked out the window at Freddy, she saw

Virginia. She was sitting on her haunches beside her father, in her beige and brown jumper, and her short no-color hair; sitting watching him, looking for all the world like a huge, devoted, cross-eyed Siamese cat.

Gloria said, "I suppose Freddy's on Milo's side."

"Oh, who's choosing up sides, honey? It hasn't come to that, has it?" She waved away some of the smoke spiraling up between them. "You know Freddy. He's always liked Milo. Freddy likes people who are different. He likes that subtle stuff Milo's always talking about, the stuff about the life cycle of insects and saints and all. You know how Freddy is. He hates the corny American Legion, hail-fel-low-well-met type!" She paused a moment before she said, "I guess I don't have to tell you he was never overly fond of you, honey. Freddy's awfully stuffy when you come right down to it."

"Stuffy?" Gloria Wealdon looked at her hard. "That's a funny word to use about Freddy."

"Well, you couldn't use it about me, could you, honey? I'm a money snob, in some ways, but money snobs are happy as long as they're not poor, and we've done all right. Freddy's different. He's a taste snob. That's why we never had a Cadillac. God knows I love those big chrome boats, love them! But Freddy thinks they're in bad taste."

"*Freddy!*" Glo said.

"Half of our arguments are about my bad taste, honey. He thinks I fill the house up with too much senseless or-namentation. You know me! I like pretty things. I like them all done up fancy. Not Freddy!"

"Well, *I* don't overdress."

Fern smiled at her. It was the same patronizing smile Gloria could remember from scores of long-past tea par-ties, sit-down dinners, coffee klatches with just the two of them; it was always the same, that smile.

Fern said, "You *under-dress,* dear."

"Is that Freddy's business?"

It was a senseless rejoinder.

"Of course it isn't his business," said Fern, "but you asked me why Freddy's stuffy where you're concerned, didn't you?"

Gloria couldn't remember. She sipped the Nescafé wordlessly.

"Honey," said Fern, "I *like* the way you are! I'm not like Freddy. I don't care what you wear, or if you belong to the Birthday Club, or whether you take the right fork at dinner, or what kind of comment you make about food, or finger bowls, or any of it! Don't you see that?"

"Freddy ... stuffy," was all Gloria could manage.

"Yes, Freddy stuffy," said Fern more sharply. "Of course he has his naïve side too. For instance, he didn't believe the part in the book about — what did you call me? Oh yes, *Fernanda.* He simply refused to believe the part about Fernanda seducing her psychoanalyst." She let her large brown eyes raise to meet Gloria's straight on. "I'm glad he didn't believe it," she said without a trace of a smile. She was angry, in fact, really angry. "It would have caused a lot of trouble for me *and* Jay."

Gloria Wealdon glanced at the clock on the kitchen shelf. It was five minutes past eleven. She was sorry the subject of Jay Mannerheim and Fern had come up, even though she knew that eventually it was inevitable. She also knew that given enough time she could reason with Fern, help Fern to see that Jay was a selfish egotist using his so-called profession (he was *not* an M.D.) for his own gain, just as Gloria had shown in *Population 12,360.* Despite the fact that Gloria Wealdon felt less and less impressed by Fern Fulton lately, Fern was probably the only friend she had in Cayuta, New York. Until she was positive that she was not going to be in Cayuta through the summer, Gloria decided she had to make an effort to stay friends with Fern.

She said, "I want to have a long talk with you about

why I used that in my book, Fern. I really do! Not now — now I haven't got time, but let's make a date to discuss it. I'd like to let my hair down with you."

"It *doesn't* look attractive in Milo's old socks," Fern answered without any humor in her tone. Then she stood up. "I'll heat more water. You have time for another cup, don't you?"

The chameleonic mood of the morning threw Gloria Wealdon off. For the first time since her arrival back in Cayuta, she felt less sure of her ground. She could not pin down Fern's attitude toward her.

"I have time for *one* more," she said. And now, Fern's huge ears seemed somehow less grotesque than ominous, like two surreptitious listening posts that had been there all the time, of course. But before she could decide what was frightening about the thought, Fern's face was cut with the familiar large smile, her voice was bright again, as she gathered up the cups and saucers. "I have some divine coffee cake. I want you to try it. New York City or no, you won't taste anything like this anywhere!"

She walked toward the kitchen, her pale yellow chiffon robe trailing along the thick amber rug.

Outside in the yard, Freddy and Virginia were still attacking the weeds by the hedge. Gloria could not help feeling sorry for Fern, naming that unattractive child with the brave hope she would turn out to be as "maidenly and pure" as *What Shall We Name the Baby?* promised a Virginia would be. Gloria remembered that Fern had once said, "It's funny, but I don't really want the baby to grow up and be some kind of wild heart-breaker. I want her to be modest and maybe a little old-fashioned, you know?" That was when "Ginny" was five, when they still believed growth would correct her eyes, and before she had developed into the slow, odd and unpopular maverick she was. It was before Fern realized the child was not going to be a heart-breaker of any kind, neither wild nor modest.

Gloria looked away from the window and back at Fern, who was standing in the doorway of the kitchen. Fern's expression startled Gloria. Her mouth was tight, her nostrils slightly flared, and her eyes narrowed for those slow seconds before she spoke. The two women looked at one another — Gloria's face puzzled, Fern's cold and hard.

Then Fern said, "It doesn't — it *won't* — do me any good to know *why* you wrote about Jay and me, Gloria. I think you've always been jealous of me. But you abused a confidence! You've made my life very difficult now. *Very* difficult! I've never been laughed at before. It's a new experience for me!"

Gloria started to protest. "But why should anyone laugh at *you*? You weren't the fool! It was Jay Mannerheim who was — "

"A fool? Jay?" Fern Fulton's mouth slid into a lopsided grin that became an unseemly sneer. "*You* may think so."

"Fern, listen — "

"You listen for once," said Fern, "I've listened to you for years! I've listened to your whining and complaining about being poor, about being a misfit, about being clumsy. I've listened to everything you've ever said, and most of it — *all* of it — was about poor little Gloria Wealdon! I felt sorry for you! All right! I was nice to you! All right! Will you just ask yourself what I ever did to deserve your using my insides for plot material? That's all! Just ask yourself that! And don't explain it to me, or apologize to me. I don't want to hear about it. I just want you to know I think it was rotten of you to write about Jay and me!"

"I'm sorry," Gloria managed to say to Fern's back.

She sat there stunned. She had never heard Fern speak so vehemently. Her impulse was to get up and run back through the fields, to escape this scene which was so completely unpredicted and unprecedented.

But as she started to move, she heard Fern's voice call:

"The coffee water is boiling." The old, easy tone. "I'm cutting the cake. It's really divine cake, honey! Come on out and jabber with me while I fix it."

Gloria Wealdon walked warily into the kitchen.

Fern, all smiles, said, "Now tell me about my New York! How'd you like it, hmm? Bygones be bygones, ah?" She poked Gloria's waist playfully with her long finger. "Who'd ever have thought our little Glo-worm would write herself a best seller!"

Four

Fernanda's husband was a dull robot, still in love with her, too insensitive to be anything but proud of and anxious over the lisping maverick they had spawned.
— FROM *Population 12,360*

Virginia Fulton yanked a clump of weeds from between the two shrubs and demanded to know why she shouldn't say such a thing.

"Because," her father answered, "threats are vulgar when there is no way of carrying them out."

He squatted beside his daughter. He remembered two days back when Milo Wealdon had dropped by to help him prune the hydrangea. Milo hadn't seemed any different at all, except during one brief interval when they were examining these very shrubs he and his daughter were working on this morning. Milo had looked at them thoughtfully for a few seconds, running his tongue along the lower lip inside his mouth, the way he did sometimes. Then he had remarked: "I'd get rid of these shrubs if I were you, Freddy."

"Are you serious? They were here when I bought this place."

"I don't care. You have to get rid of them. They're lycium halimifoliums. I suppose that doesn't mean anything to you."

"What's wrong with them?"

"The popular name for them is Matrimony Vine. They have an unquenchable desire for conquest. They have these underground suckers that can just take over the whole place! You can't eradicate them by cutting them down or grubbing them out! Matrimony Vine — that's the right name for them, all right!"

"And I should get rid of them?"

"You have to kill them, Freddy."

Milo spoke those words with such emphasis that he broke the stubby black pencil he held in his hands. It was hard for Freddy to keep his mind on the rest of their conversation. All the while Milo discussed the effectiveness of Trichlorophenoxyacetic Acid sprays and Dichorophenoxyacetic Acid sprays, Freddy thought of the way Milo's big hands had snapped the piece of short lead pencil, of the way Milo had said, "Matrimony Vine — that's the right name for them!" Maybe Freddy was just projecting; maybe he was just trying to imagine how he would feel if his wife had published that best seller.

Virginia Fulton was sixteen, medium height, plump, with muscular legs, frizzy brown hair, a freckled nose and corrective glasses. She squinted at the sun from behind the thick black frames and said, "Just the same I feel like feeding her some of this stuff!" She shook the small can which she held in her hand.

"Well, I'm afraid we'll have to settle for killing mere weeds this morning, Ginny. Unless you can come up with a better idea for murdering Mrs. Wealdon. Herbicides aren't dependable. She'd probably suffer little more than a belly ache."

Freddy Fulton stood and stretched. He had been a very handsome man once. There were still traces of this in his

height, his broad shoulders, the thick crop of coal-colored
hair, the piercing dark eyes and the good rugged profile.
But at thirty-eight he had developed a paunch, the sort
that made his stance sag, and his jowls were heavy now
and flaccid. He was still impressive, partly because he
was so well-tailored, mostly because he had such an air
of self-confidence.

Fulton was not at all displeased with the figure he cut,
and when he had read Gloria Wealdon's portrayal of him
as the anxious father of a lisping daughter and the fanat-
ically devoted husband of a wife who was busy debauching
her psychoanalyst, he had guffawed aloud. He remembered that he had been sitting up in bed reading the book,
and that Fern, opposite him in her bed, had demanded:
"What's so funny, Freddy?"

He really pitied Fern. He wondered if that was what his
whole attitude toward her had evolved into.

"Oh, I don't know," he had answered. "Poor old Milo."
He had closed the novel abruptly, so that she would not
know he was reading the seduction scene between Fernanda and her analyst.

"Not poor Virginia?" Fern had snapped. "Not poor
Min Stewart?" she had added. Freddy knew she meant
— *not poor me?* Fern had slapped cold cream across her
face with an angry gesture, and continued, "After all,
your own daughter was maligned in that book. *And* your
best friend. Where would you be without Min? Who put
up the money for your loan when all the banks refused
credit?"

"All right," he had said. "Poor Virginia. Poor Min."

"But you don't really mean it, do you?"

"No," Freddy had admitted, "I don't. Ginny can do
circles around Gloria Wealdon any day; so can Min Stewart. Neither one of them gives a damn what that idiot
wrote about them."

Fern had shouted, "Sometimes I think you know less

about the human mechanism than anyone I've ever encountered!"

The storm warnings were posted. Whenever Fern began
talking about "the human mechanism" at the top of her
lungs, the first rag of civility was about to be ripped away.

"I don't want to argue, Fern," Freddy had answered in
a mild tone.

"Don't *I* know it!" Fern laughed sarcastically. "You
want to keep your hostility all bottled up inside of you.
You'll find other ways to punish me, won't you, Fred?"

"The idea of punishing you," Freddy replied truthfully,
"bores me." He felt like adding: "As does your new vocabulary," but he checked himself.

At the last Rotary Club meeting, he had made the same
complaint to Jay Mannerheim. Jay had answered that all
patients tossed around psychological words in the beginning.

"In the *beginning!*" Freddy had laughed. "Fern's been
laid out on your couch for two and a half years now!"

Jay had nodded sadly. "I know it seems like a long time
to the layman, but it's really a relatively short time. It's a
big job unraveling thirty-three years."

Freddy grimaced. "Fern's thirty-seven, not thirty-three.
I can't see what good you can do if she won't even tell
you the truth!"

"She will … in time," said Jay. He had knocked the
dottle from his pipe and continued in a confidential tone.
"Freddy — about Virginia. You know crossed eyes, in
many cases, are due to some hereditary anatomical weakness, but I don't think that's so in Ginny's case. I mean
there's no history of it in either Fern's background *or*
yours."

"I agree," Freddy had said.

"No one is responsible for her condition," Jay had
added, "and no one should *feel* responsible."

"Does anyone?"

"Fulton, do you know what I'm trying to get across?"

"What?"

Momentarily Jay had studied Freddy's bland face. Then stuffing his pipe in his pocket, he had said: "You must be punishing Fern for something, Freddy."

"You've been reading Gloria Wealdon's version of Fern's version of life at the Fultons'," Freddy'd laughed.

"Except that Gloria Wealdon's version includes one devoted husband."

"And one debauched psychoanalyst."

Jay had shaken his head. "That part *was* rather pathetic. Patients, particularly women, enjoy imagining that they have the ability to seduce their analysts. It's a little private daydream. It was sad that it had to be brought out in the open."

"Even sadder," Freddy had said, "that they *don't* have the ability."

"I suppose that wouldn't bother you."

Freddy had told him honestly, "I'd feel as though Fern's analysis was a better investment under those circumstances. At least she'd be getting *something* for my money, besides a lot of psychological jargon she's not mentally equipped to grasp."

Standing abruptly, Jay Mannerheim had looked down at Freddy Fulton with a serious expression to his countenance. "I'm not out selling my wares, Fulton, but a remark such as that makes me feel obliged to suggest that *you* could use a little therapy yourself. Have you ever considered analysis?"

Freddy had told him that he already knew the art of being unhappy intelligently.

Freddy Fulton liked Jay Mannerheim. Of course he was terribly pompous and something of an ass, but Freddy felt he meant well, and in some instances he probably actually *did* help people. If he was getting nowhere with Fern, it was because Fern would never admit the truth.

She had long ago stopped admitting it to herself, so why should she tell Jay Mannerheim about it.

If Freddy were as prone to label things as Fern was, he would label the matter "Fern's mental block." For even to Freddy, Fern had never made reference to the year 1953, except to berate Hollywood on occasion for giving Audrey Hepburn an Oscar that year.

In the year 1953 Freddy Fulton fell in love. Freddy was like a lot of people who had married very young and out-grown their mates. Like the others, Freddy, after he had met Edwina Dare, began to distinguish between the act of loving someone and the experience of being *in* love with someone. He had loved Fern; he supposed in some crazy way he would always love Fern — such was the complexity of marital love; but he was *in* love with Edwina Dare. Wouldn't he always be?

Still, in 1953 he had let her move away from Cayuta; he had not tried to stop her.

He could still remember the painful night when he had made his decision. Fern had gone to the bedroom, while Freddy sat in the dark in their cream-colored living room. He sat there for hours, debating, reasoning, weeping; he sat there like a man in a dream, who knew how beautiful the dream was, but also knew, the way sometimes a man does on the thin edge of sleep, that soon he would have to wake up. When finally he decided he could not bring himself to abandon Fern and Ginny and go off blissfully with his Edwina, he got up and went into the bedroom to tell Fern. He expected to find her waiting there, tortured, the same way he had been, by the thought that their marriage hung by a hair. When he opened the door, he saw her sitting by the radio, in tears, and for the first time since their trouble had started he had felt compassion for her, he had felt he had made the right decision. Crossing the room, he held out his arms to her, intending to say something comforting, something like *there, there, now;*

it's going to be all right between us, Fern. He had been prevented from speaking immediately by Fern's sudden wailing.

"Audrey Hepburn is no actress!" she had cried. "Gawd, Freddy, remember the old pictures? Remember Ida Lupino in 'The Hard Way'? We saw it in New York City that Easter, remember? Ida Lupino could act; still can! She deserves an Oscar, but *this one!*"

It was Ginny he had put his arms around that night, holding her sleepy-eyed in her pajamas. It was Ginny he murmured to: "It's going to be all right."

Now, six years later, Freddy Fulton was grateful for the fact Fern was seeing Jay Mannerheim three afternoons a week. Ever since Gloria Wealdon's book was published, Fern had been carrying on in an astonishing way — praising Gloria one moment, damning her the next. Her moods, lately, were never predictable.

Freddy would be buckling his galoshes in the kitchen in the morning, on his way to the plant, when suddenly Fern would walk in and announce: "I never told Gloria Wealdon you idolized me! She made that up! I don't need anyone idolizing me! Believe you me, I had all of *that* I could use when I was a girl. Why, the boys at Miss Bryan's Dancing School used to break their necks racing across that waxed ballroom floor to get me for the opening waltz. I think I told you that Jack Fowler — he's a big man in stocks and bonds now, lives up in Fairfield County — Jack Fowler broke his collarbone right there on Miss Bryan's waxed floor, racing across to get me for the opener!"

"I'm glad to hear it," Freddy would answer.

That would be all there was to it, until the next time.

The next time, Freddy and Fern and Ginny might be watching television, and Freddy and Ginny would laugh at something they thought was corny on the screen. Then again it would happen; a *different* version. Fern would say: "It isn't good to be smug about what you *may* think is corny, Virginia. Some people can't afford to be smug. Your father is a little over-protective. He'll sit there and laugh with you at the pretty girls who can't act on the television, without ever explaining that pretty girls have the upper hand in the world, whether they're talented or not! Your father won't tell you the simple facts of life, Virginia. Even Gloria Wealdon can figure out the simple facts of life. She told the truth in that novel. That's why people are so indignant!"

Freddy — and Virginia, too — became gradually accustomed to Fern's irrational outbursts, so both were prepared for this morning's incident.

After breakfast, Fern had said, "Listen, Gloria Wealdon is coming down here to have coffee with me. So *she* thinks! I think I'll slam the door in her face! And if either of you speak to her, I'm not going to speak to you!"

Freddy had sighed tiredly.

"I mean it, Freddy!"

He had said to his daughter, "C'mon, Ginny, let's get those Matrimonial Vines."

"I'm with you, Dad," his daughter had grinned.

As they were leaving the back door, they had nearly collided with Gloria Wealdon. Freddy had held Ginny's arm tightly and whispered, "Try to please your mother, Ginny, and don't speak to her."

"Don't worry," Ginny had answered. "I don't have anything to say to Gloria Wealdon."

Freddy had been slightly surprised at Virginia's bitter tone. He and Ginny had laughed so much over *Population 12,360* that he had not anticipated that kind of reaction. He was pondering this when Gloria Wealdon nearly knocked them over, waving and calling "Hi" on her way into their house. He was beginning to wonder, for the first time, if his daughter actually had taken the novel seriously.

His wife's voice had interrupted his musing: "Well, hi, Glo!" she called from the steps. "Gee, I'm glad you could come!"

Maybe, Freddy had thought, Fern is really and truly cracking up.

Beside him now in the Fulton backyard, Freddy heard his daughter say, "Well?"

"Well, what?"

"You've been dreaming ... I asked you if it wouldn't kill Gloria Wealdon if I used the *whole* can?

There's arsenic in it, isn't there?"

"Yes," Freddy said. "There is."

"I could write a sequel to her book," said Ginny. "I could call it *Population, 12,359.*"

Freddy chuckled. Then again he wondered if it *could* be possible that the novel had hurt Ginny.

Everyone in Cayuta, he supposed, knew who the lisping teen-ager was supposed to be. Ginny herself had once or twice pretended to lisp in fun, after she had read the book. She had teased Freddy about their closeness too, often satirizing an old song by singing:

> *"We be-long*
> *to a mu-tu-al,*
> *ad-mir-a-tion*
> *so-ci-ety — my fath-er and me."*

Once, when Fern was getting ready for her appointment with Jay, Ginny had said, "Will the kindly psychoanalyst be able to resist the devastating Mrs. Frederick Fulton during *this* session? Tune in tomorrow — "

Fern had cut her off by screaming, "Virginia! Don't you ever, *ever* speak that way again!"

"What do you want her to do?" Freddy had asked Fern later that evening when they were alone. "Take that book seriously?"

"Doesn't she even know when someone's made a fool of her?" said Fern.

"She knows someone's tried," Freddy had answered, "and she knows how to laugh off a bad joke."

"Ginny's afraid to show *you* her true feelings," Fern had begun shouting again. "You expect her to behave the way you do. Old, unflinching, unfeeling Freddy — old Ironsides!"

"Don't raise your voice, Fern!"

"Freddy, dammit all, people *raise* their voices when their houses are on fire. And our house is on fire! If I want to holler *fire,* I will! One of these days Ginny is going to holler fire too!"

At the time, Freddy had dismissed the whole idea of his inhibiting Ginny by his own example of durability as just another of Fern's notions. But that Saturday morning when Ginny began all the teasing talk about poisoning Gloria Wealdon, Freddy wondered just what kind of a joke it was. He remembered Jay Mannerheim's cliché, *No one ever jokes,* and he thought that it simply was not like Ginny to indulge in such obvious, trivial humor. One of the things he had always admired about Virginia was her subtlety; another was her poise and dignity. To Freddy, she was a remarkably intact personality. Apart from being his daughter, whom he loved, she was a human being he admired and respected.

He turned to Ginny and said, "Tell me something, honey, would you really like to see Mrs. Wealdon dead?"

"Yes, a little."

"I wonder why. It doesn't seem much like you, Ginny."

"I feel sorry for Mr. Wealdon." She stood up. She pushed her glasses back up on her nose and squinted at the sunlight. "I keep thinking of the time those bulb mites got at his tulip bulbs. He was furious! I was with him the afternoon he soaked the bulbs in nicotine sulphate. I thought he was going to cry, he was so furious."

"It wouldn't do him much good to cry over his wife's book, Ginny."

"It's not that. It's just that it's too bad a man like that had to marry someone like her!"

"Someday you'll discover that people usually deserve each other, Ginny."

"I know your theories on that subject."

"Do you agree with me?"

"I have always ... but Mr. Wealdon doesn't deserve her. It was different with you. There was Edwina to make up for things mother lacked."

"It was never that your mother lacked something, Virginia. It was just that after I met Edwina, I wanted more. Not from your mother. Just from Edwina — her particular kind of gentleness."

"I know all that. I didn't mean to bring it up. It's just that I feel sorry for Mr. Wealdon. He doesn't deserve a woman like her."

"Maybe he does. Maybe he wants to protect a woman, watch out for her. You know how solicitous he is with his plants and everything. Well, he's got a handful in Gloria Wealdon. I don't know anyone besides your mother who's ever felt even lukewarm toward that woman."

"Mother was sorry for her too."

"Yes, I think so. She'd deny it, but I think so. Your mother's always had a soft spot for people like that."

"Poor mother."

"Yes," said Fulton. "She's been very upset."

Virginia Fulton sighed, kicking the small pile of weeds at her feet. After a moment, she smiled. "Dad, would you like some hot coffee?"

"Yes, Ginny."

"I can sneak in the back way and get some for us. I'll bring it out here in the old thermos."

Freddy watched her run up the lawn. She was so quick and bright and good-natured; so intuitive, too. He found himself thinking for a moment of what her grandfather used to say: "*God gave handicaps only to the highest types. Little minds are subdued and ruined by them; great minds are challenged and made by them.*"

He looked after her, and then he experienced the wonderful feeling a parent does, when, for no particular reason, at some random interval, on no especial day, he suddenly has a heart full of pride, when he observes his child in a simple, everyday situation.

Smiling, Freddy Fulton knelt down by the Matrimony Vine and began looking around for the can of herbicide.

Five

His name was Will: Big Will she always called him in her mind, and she always saw him looking at her with a certain cockiness to his expression, a certain snideness, as though he could read her thoughts, and knew what she called him to herself — Big Will.
— FROM *Population 12,360*

Stanley Secora sat on the green bench at the bus stop on the corner of Genesee Street and Alden Avenue.

A new Buick pulled over, and the owner pointed toward downtown with his finger and beckoned questioningly with his eyes at Stanley. Stanley shook his head. "No thanks!" The Buick's owner, an attorney, waved and went on.

That made the sixth person who had offered Stanley a ride. Stanley didn't need a ride. In fifteen or twenty minutes he would get up and walk down Alden Avenue to the Wealdons, for his appointment with Mrs. Wealdon. But meanwhile, Stanley liked sitting on the green bench while people stopped and offered him a lift. There was no doubt about his popularity. Every single summer since the war he had more lawns to cut than he needed, and in the winter he had an assistant help him with the walks he was asked to shovel. Evenings when he came home from his regular job, working as a stock clerk for Freddy Fulton, the "Y" switchboard operator invariably had two or three messages for him. He would get painting jobs, planting jobs. He even did plumbing work once out at the Riford summer camp. All kinds of work would come his way in a never-ending stream. Someone once made the remark that in Cayuta, New York, people never used the expression "let George do it"; people said, "call up Stanley." Stanley liked to remember that.

Stanley liked the way people counted on him. He always had. When he was a kid, growing up in the Kantogee County Orphans' Home, on the outskirts of Cayuta, he was the best lawn-raker, ashcan-emptier, bed-maker, floor-mopper, and errand-runner of anyone in the Home. In the army, he never minded K.P. He didn't even hate latrine duty. Work was work; a job had to be done. That was the way Stanley felt about it.

Sometimes when you did a job well (like last week when he helped lay Sandran in the Meens' kitchen, and Mrs. Meen kept saying afterward, Oh, it's so nice! It really is nice! Oh, my, Stanley, thank you!) your satisfaction was in the reaction of other people. Delighted astonishment, in Mrs. Meen's case; a direct and forthright compliment from someone like Dr. Mannerheim; a dollar pressed into his palm by Freddy Fulton; or from Min Stewart the offer of a cold beer which he could have out on the back steps in the summer, or in the warm kitchen in the winter.

During the war, of course, it was best of all. There were medals, but it wasn't just the medals — it was before the medals. It was jumping out of that foxhole with mud on your face and some kind of crazy wings on your big, dirt-clogged fatigue boots, pulling the thing on the hand grenade and shouting "Yah! Yah! Yah!", as though you were just routing out some stupid crows from a corn patch, instead of Germans.

"Boy, you sure have got guts!" someone would say.

"Man, are you out of your G.I. mind! The chances you take!" Someone else.

And once an officer who didn't even know a single thing about Stanley Secora took one long look at him, and said he would be good front-line material. A thing like that could make Stanley's day.

Stanley never knew where he got his nerve, but he knew he had it.

Every time he did something to win himself another medal, he knew no fear. He even began to believe nothing could touch him, not a bullet, not a mine, not a bomb — nothing, if he, Stanley Secora, had the bull by the horns. That belief kept him returning to the front; and ultimately returned him to an astounded, but nonetheless wildly pleased Cayuta.... Stanley Secora, the third-most-decorated soldier of World War II. The American Legion Band met his train. Min Stewart's husband, who was still alive then, offered him a permanent job at the drug store (which he would have accepted if it were not for the fact he would have to work alongside Louie Stewart) and the Knights of Columbus had a Stanley Secora Night, with a huge bigger-than-life photograph of him all blown up and wired around the basketball net in the basement of Saint Alphonsus Church.

Stanley sat on the green bench that morning in May, smiling to recall those days. What was that song playing over and over that summer he was a hero? Got no something, got no hum, dum de dum de? Then he remembered. Got no dia-monds, got no rings, but I've got plenty of ev-ry thing: I got the sun in the morning and the moon at night. That was it. It always reminded Stanley of good old 1946.

Beside Stanley on the bench were two boxes, one containing two pieces of coconut ice (candy he had made himself) and the other the first three chapters of his novel. The candy, he realized, was a romantic inspiration, and he felt a trifle sheepish about going behind Mr. Wealdon's back. He could not justify his intentions toward Gloria Wealdon; he no longer tried. He was sick, silly, down-to-his-toes in love with the author of *Population 12,360,* and that was that. The only thing that *did* make him feel better about his date with her that noon, was the fact that Love was not his sole motivation. There was his novel, which he wanted her to read; he called it *A Vet's Memories.*

Stanley Secora, six months ago, would never have dreamed of getting anyplace with Milo Wealdon's wife. Women (when he thought about them *that* way) had always been a source of painful embarrassment to Stanley. It was because he felt clumsy and ugly in their presence. The summer of 1946, when he was at his peak, wearing his uniform around Cayuta with his medals pinned to it, some of the Polish girls from the Falcon's Ladies Lodge had crushes on him. This did nothing to inspire confidence in Stanley. They were all fat and pimply and left-over, and instead of being flattered by their giggling and blushing in his presence, he felt conspicuous, as though he had cast his lot with them. It made him feel as though he were a war hero for nothing, and there was the slight suspicion that if he had not been a war hero, even those homely wallflowers would not have him.

Population 12,360 changed all that. When he read Gloria Wealdon's novel, he saw himself in a new light. He was Will, the husky, somewhat awkward character who did odd jobs around the town. He was Will, and the heroine used to watch him mow her lawn from her window, and wonder what would happen if she called him into the house and showed him her sheerest black negligee.

Stanley could almost remember one part word for word:

> *The sprinkler was turned on the hot, August-parched summer lawn. Will wore no shirt. His back was browned from the sun, and as he pushed the mower along the part behind the sprinkler, tiny blades of grass were caught in the cuffs of his worn levis. Now and then he stopped and flicked them away, or mopped his brow with an old soiled handkerchief he kept in his back trousers pocket. He looked big and perspiring, all down his back perspiring, like some kind of huge work animal who would do almost anything you told him to do. She thought of calling him, of telling him to come inside. She thought of saying: "I want you to do something for me, Will. I want you to pick me up and carry me over to that couch, and then I want you to rip my clothes off me and make me naked."*

Just thinking about it made Stanley's pulse race.

He flipped his wrist up so he could see his watch. It was eleven-thirty. He had fifteen minutes more to wait. Near his wrist there was a bandage; he had burned himself while he was making the candy. It was painful, but he thought about it the way he had thought about his battle wounds during the war. It was part of the reward attached to winning; the only difference was that in this case he bore the scars of the battle before the battle was fought. There probably wouldn't even be a battle, Stanley Secora decided happily. With Gloria Wealdon as his objective, victory was certain. He felt euphoric, and, like any good soldier, not at all brave yet.

Six

*Miles was not violent, not about anything. The
word violence to him was like ham to an orthodox
Jew. Sure, there was such a thing, but he had only
heard about it; never had a taste of it, nor any appetite for it...*
— FROM *Population 12,360*

In the dream Gloria was dressed like Cinderella.

"I'm leaving you," she said, "unless you can prove
you're the real Prince, and my literary agent is not. If you
are," she continued, "you'll be able to wear this shoe."

She held a space shoe in her hand. It was as big as a
bread box.

Then there were the shots, one after the other, *bang,
bang, bang!* ...

Milo jumped to his feet. He stood in the living room,
momentarily dazed. The dream was done. The banging
continued.

Then he realized that someone was pulling on the front
screen door, which he had locked just after his migraine
had started. He had lain on the couch, intending to rest
for only a few minutes, but he must have slept for twenty.

The clock on the mantle read eleven-forty. As he started
toward the screen door, he could not deny that there was
a certain sense of gratification in him, accomplished
through the dream. He could not help it; it had started at
the dream's point when he had pulled the trigger on the
gun. Only it was not a gun in the dream; it was an arsenate
of lead bomb, the kind he had used last April to rid the
iris of borers. But it had worked like a gun would; it had
shot Gloria. He had awakened as she fell forward, clutch-

ing at her stomach.

Over and over in the past weeks, he had dreamed of killing his wife. The stuff of his dreams was theatrical, as though his unconscious mind were putting forth its whole imaginative effort to stage Gloria's murder with every bit of uncanny creativity possessed by Milo. Once, last week, he had dreamed that Gloria was Saint Febronia. He had seen the angry mobs pull seventeen teeth from her mouth, tear her breasts off, and ultimately burn her. Another time, Milo had dreamed he was bent over a proud bi-colored narcissus in some dream garden, when he noticed that the tissues of the plant seemed soft and rotted. At the moment in the dream when he said, "This plant will die. It has Bortrytis Bulb Rot!" the yellow and the white of the flower faded together and became skin and the skin became Gloria's face.

At the same time that Milo felt the gratification he felt sick in his heart. It was the same sickness that overtook him whenever he was reminded, in his gardening, or in his study of the saints' lives, that the whole living world constituted a colossal cannibalism, a holocaust in which life continues only at the cost of death. Man lives because of the sacrifice of plants and animals, and in his own turn is a sacrifice to the birds and the worms, or to the bacilli which effect his death. Gloria, in his dreams, was sacrificed to his inmost hostile fantasies, just as he had been to hers in her novel. He smiled forlornly at the thought, and then found himself in his front hall, facing an even more forlorn fellow.

Unlatching the screen door, Milo said: "Come on in, Stanley. She isn't home yet. I suspect she'll be along in a while."

"I thought you'd be at the track meet," said Stanley, as he waddled past Milo. He was perspiring, and his glasses were steamed. Under his arm he carried two boxes; one small, like a jewelers box, the other with SPHINX TYPE-WRITER PAPER, ESQUIRE BOND printed across it. He followed Milo into the living room, bumping into a chair en route. His face turned a brilliant red as he mumbled an inane apology to the furniture.

"I'm going to the meet in a very short while," Milo told him.

About the only way Milo could communicate with Stanley Secora was to demonstrate his own ineptness. Milo himself stumbled as he bent over to pick up his sport coat from the couch. He said something equally inane: "Whoops-a-crazy-daisy."

Both men laughed, and blushed, fidgeting nervously.

Milo remembered how he had quite inadvertently sculptured Saint Felix of Cantalice in a way which bore a very good likeness to Stanley. Even Gloria, who commented less and less on Milo's sculptures, noticed the resemblance. She had said, "Migod, this one looks like Stanley Secora. Some saint he'd make, the blundering ox!"

"In a sense," Milo had explained, "St. Felix *was* an oaf, but I really hadn't intended to draw a parallel."

"You talk about them as if they were people you knew. How do you know St. Felix was like Secora?"

"I don't. I never said they were alike. It was just an impression I wasn't even aware of.... But it's not too far wrong."

"Well, you better get Saint Felix on the phone; the windows in the front need cleaning."

"Saint Felix," said Milo, "was always apologizing for himself — the way Stanley does. You know, as though he's in the way. Felix wore a shirt studded with iron spikes, and he never wore shoes, and if anyone did something mean to him, he always said, 'I pray God that you may become a saint.'"

"Some kind of masochist, if you ask me," said Gloria.

"Most of the saints were, when you think about it."

"I'd rather think about the Marquis de Sade," said Gloria. "That's what makes horse races, ah, Milo?"

At those times, Milo Wealdon felt no streak of hatred in him toward her. He was *all* hatred, with a streak of forgiveness in him toward Gloria, so tiny that it was like a sliver in the backside of a rhinoceros. Still, his hatred was impotent. He was left quaking with it, helpless. It was like a migraine. He just had to wait until it went away.

Stanley Secora's voice cut into his reverie.

"Yes," Stanley repeated, "I thought you'd be over at the high school, Mr. Wealdon."

"Oh, I'm going there," Milo said. "Mrs. Wealdon ought to be along any minute."

Stanley sank into the folds of the couch. "Tempus fugit," he smiled.

Milo was about to say something compulsive and idiotic like "It certainly does fugit," but both of them were saved from the preposterous conversation by Gloria's sudden appearance.

To Milo she said, "Well, I hear you've won the Fultons over to your side! Playing the part of the great all-suffering husband, ready to forgive me anything!" She punctuated her sentence with that little *Psssss* noise she made whenever she wanted to ridicule something.

She said to Stanley, "It must be mental telepathy, Stanley. I was just noticing that our car could use a good bath."

"Stanley is here to discuss writing with you," Milo told her.

"Don't get that supercilious tone in your voice, J.C.," she answered sarcastically, standing legs spread and arms akimbo, with her head cocked to one side. "You're *such* a martyr, aren't you, *dear* good Milo?"

Stanley was squirming in his seat, his fat hands twisting the manuscript box flap in an anguished manner.

Milo realized something had gone wrong at the Fultons.

Again, he felt the tentacles of pity reach out from him, felt his anger and embarrassment fade. He wanted to say: how sorry I am, Glo; at the same time he pictured the benign face of Freddy Fulton, and thought how quiet and subtle their friendship had always been. Only a few days ago, when Milo had felt an almost overwhelming urge to talk to someone about his plot for revenge, he had gone through the shortcut in the fields to visit with Freddy. He had stood beside him before the lycium halimifoliums, and they *had* talked, but not a word about his plot. Freddy's unshakable dignity had sustained Milo in that moment of weakness, had saved Milo from the vulgar experience of unburdening himself to another person. He had never stopped admiring Freddy for the way he had handled himself in his affair with Edwina Dare. Even Gloria had never gotten wind of that chapter in the Fultons' life; so few in Cayuta had. There were rumors among some of the town's businessmen at the time, but the girl's name was not known. Sometimes Milo wondered whether it was a fluke, or an act of faith on Freddy's part, that Freddy did something that told Milo who she was.

He had done it one evening back in 1953. He had taken Milo aside at one of the country club buffets, and had said that he wanted his advice about something. He had a friend, he said, who was a Catholic. He wanted to give this friend a medal of some kind, as a gift. A sort of going-away present.

"You know about the saints and all that, Milo," said he. "What could you give someone who was around books all the time?"

"St. Catharine is the saint of learned men," Milo had told him.

"Isn't there a saint for someone who sells books?"

Edwina Dare, the girl who worked at The Book Mart ... plain, quiet, nice Edwina Dare. Milo had often been waited on by her in the Mart, when he ordered the Peterson field guide series, or the texts for his classes in skin and scuba diving. Memory is an uncanny confederate. He could remember then an afternoon out near Hubbard's nursery, on the outskirts of Cayuta, when he had come across Freddy's Buick, parked and empty. Milo had pulled up and parked beside it, and as he was getting out to see if he could find Freddy, he found him, sitting on a log just at the entrance to the woods, with Edwina Dare. They had exchanged pleasantries. Freddy had made no attempt to explain what he was doing there in mid-afternoon with Edwina, and Milo somehow had not thought that peculiar. He had been only slightly surprised at seeing Edwina with Freddy, yet not surprised enough to dwell on it. Perhaps the most peculiar part about the whole incident was that later in the day, when Milo and Gloria had a drink in the backyard with Freddy and Fern, neither man referred to the meeting. It was as though their silence on the matter was simply understood. And yet, until Freddy asked Milo about the saint who sold books, it never occurred to Milo that Freddy was deeply in love with Edwina Dare.

Milo had simply answered, "St. John Port Latin is the saint you want."

"Thanks," Freddy had said. He had clapped Milo across the shoulder, and they had gone back to join the others.

That had been all there was to it.

Now, Milo supposed, Freddy was somehow making it obvious to Gloria that he did not approve of her, making it obvious, undoubtedly, through Fern. It was a vote of confidence in Milo, but like all of them he had received in the past, it made Milo want to protect Glo, protect her even from his own inevitable pity.

He said nothing more to her. He walked from the living room with his sport coat hung across his shoulder, leaving her with Secora, thinking for the first time that day that he did not want any revenge, that, God help him, he was all she had, wasn't he? The word Pitts came to mind, but he thought only of seedy old peach and olive pits, and of all things left-over and unwanted, things no one loved, and his anxiety and bitterness knew a respite in sadness and sympathy, which in fact had always been an asylum for him.

Seven

Will began to be an obsession with her. When would they be alone together? Wasn't she actually afraid of him? And the thought that she could be really afraid of any man made her tingle all over.
— FROM *Population 12,360*

Gloria reached into her frontier pants for her package of cigarettes. She lit one and blew smoke from her nostrils as she strode across to the picture window, feeling quite a lot like Bette Davis. Except for the stomach ache, another one of her damn nervous stomach aches. She could not forget Fern's remark about Freddy being stuffy — the reason he was (how had she put it?) never "overly-fond of *you*, dear." That's rich, she thought, oh that *is* rich. Freddy Fulton stuffy!

"And so," she said as she stared out at the Japanese quince, "you want to be a writer, Stanley." She sucked in smoke, turning then in a fast movement, facing him.

Stanley Secora looked as though he were going to faint. Instead, he nodded. He was perspiring and his face was the color of a lobster. Gloria thought of the hero of Victor Hugo's novel about Notre Dame — Quasimodo, the deaf, deformed, grotesque bell-ringer of the cathedral, who was in love with the beautiful Esmeralda.

She said, "What have you written?"

"A book. My war memories, Mrs. Wealdon." He held

out the manuscript box. A timid smile crossed his countenance. "Don't be nervous, m'am."

"Nervous, Stanley?"

"I'm sorry. I mean, I can't thank you enough for giving
up this time to read it."

"You mean read it right now?" She laughed. "I just
can't sit down and start to read it now."

She took the manuscript box and placed it on the end
table. "I have a date for lunch."

Stanley fumbled in the pocket of his sweater jacket until
he found the other box, the small one. "I brought you
some candy."

"Is this a bribe? I *do* have a date for lunch."

She felt sorry for him, and irritated that she did.

"Oh, it's no bribe, Mrs. Wealdon. Oh no, m'am." He
shuffled his feet and held out the small box.

"Coconut ice. Your favorite, I heard."

He had the top of the box off, and when he unfolded
the tissue paper there were two pieces of candy.

"Not now, Stanley. Put them by your manuscript."

"You don't want any, Mrs. Wealdon?"

"Not before lunch…. About the book, I'd be glad to
read it. You'll have to give me plenty of time."

"I made that candy myself, Mrs. Wealdon," said Stanley,
backing into a chair.

"I appreciate it. Thank you. I'll have it when I come
home from lunch. For dessert. I really *do* have a lunch
date, and I'm in a hurry."

He looked blankly at her.

"I'll read it within the next week," she said.

He rubbed his hands together, and she noticed the bandages. "Did you have an accident?"

"I burned myself, making the candy."

"Sorry."

"I wish I knew if you liked it. I wish you'd have some."

"I have to dress now, Stanley."

She ground out her cigarette emphatically. "I'm in a hurry."

"I'll take it back," he said, "if you don't want it, then I'll — "

She was suddenly exasperated. She whirled and, very nearly shouting, said, "Good heavens, Stanley, don't behave so stupidly! I'll eat your candy and I'll read your book, but you must go right now!"

Perhaps she really had shouted, for, without saying another word, Stanley fled.

"When does he arrive, Gloria?" Milo's voice said behind her.

"When does who arrive?" She pulled her shirttail out of her pants, began pulling the socks out of her hair, and started walking toward the bathroom. "I thought you'd gone."

"You know who. Your literary agent."

"Oh? So you *are* aware that he's coming?" She bent and turned on the water in the tub. "He'll be here tonight."

"We ought to have a talk before then, Gloria."

"We're having one now, aren't we. Just carry on," she said, kicking off her space shoes.

"I think you could have given Stanley a little more time than you did."

"I'm sure you think that, Milo. You feel obliged to be sweet and kind and tolerant of any creep who rides up on a bicycle. You married me because *I* was a creep. Was. Past tense. Or didn't you think I'd figured that out, Milo?"

Milo's head was throbbing again.

He said, "Why do we have to argue this way? There are certain things that need to be said between us. Can't we say them in a quiet way?"

"Whisper, if you'd like," she answered, grinning up at him. She flung her pants and bra into the tub. It had always annoyed him that Gloria did her laundry while she took her bath, soaping her stockings and her underwear right along with her arms and legs.

"Are you going to leave me?" he said. He looked at her, at all of her. It was pathetic the way her hips had spread, the way her figure had surrendered itself to middle age, though she was only thirty-three. She had stretch marks, and she was flabby-thighed and too soft.

"Do you want me to?" She tested the water with her toe, turning her back on him.

He thought how he would like to take his knee and ram her rear end with it, so that she'd go head-first into the tub.

"No," he said sincerely, "I don't want you to."

"And if I do?" she said. "Hand me the soap."

"Maybe I'd kill myself." He didn't know why he said it, or why he laughed. He had intended not to answer that question at all, but there you were; the answer had just come out. He handed her the soap.

She eased herself into the hot water. Pretty soon her skin would get very red; her heart would race. She always took baths too hot for anyone. They made her weak after. In the beginning of their marriage, he had liked to make love to her when she was fresh from the bath. He had liked it if she was still a little moist, and smelling of the talcum she used. He used to sit on the top of the toilet seat watching her bathe, and it would excite him, and he would take her when she stepped from the tub into the towel he held waiting.

Now he stood there by the sink, and her breasts looked like great hams, not exciting.

"How would you kill yourself?" she said.

"I have a pill."

"You'll need more than one. Ouch! Hot!"

"No, I'll only need the one. It's very effective." It was strychnine. He had used it to rout the large field rats from the city dump last year, when he had accepted the position of chairman of the dump clearing project. Strychnine was a product of the Quaker Button tree, native to the East Indies, a most violent poison, which Milo even hated to use on rats. How had he ever become involved in this conversation with Gloria?

She seemed unfazed. "I'd jump, if I were you." She soaped herself vigorously. "Pills are not infallible in the age of the stomach pump and mobile oxygen tank. I'd jump. You just pick out a Jim-dandy hotel, ask for a room on the courtyard, on the nineteenth floor, have yourself a deliciously expensive dinner — on the house," she chuckled, smoothing the washcloth along her arm, "have a couple of splits of champagne — and then whoosh!" She raised her hand and let the washcloth splash into the water. "Fini! Au reservoir, and all that!"

Milo decided that it was unbelievably pathetic that Gloria, in her conception of a suicide, should include the minor triumph of getting out of paying the dinner check. He sighed.

"'For *Miles,*'" she said, "'was endlessly sighing away his existence, in hallways by coat racks, on gravel driveways on his way to — '"

"We'll have the talk another time," he said.

Gloria shrugged. "Close the door after you, there's a draft!"

She spent the rest of the time in the tub, imagining how amused Pitts Ralei would be when she discussed Milo with him that evening. Pitts had a theory that the European male, like himself, was prone to falling in love with angelic-looking women who turned out in reality to be sluts; the American male, on the other hand, was susceptible to half-clad, very sexy, Martini-drinking females who were actually by nature quite virginal.

"You see it all the time in the movies," he would say. "Our Frenchman with his Jeanne d'Arc who sells her flesh by night in Montmartre, and your American with his Marilyn Monroe who's really only working in that road-house to support her three kids, and never allows a man so much as a passing pinch on the buttocks."

Pitts was so darned clever, Gloria thought. Whenever he said, "*Very* good," in response to an observation Gloria made, she felt manifestly erudite. Tonight, she planned to tell him about Milo. He never really seemed to understand the way Milo was. She thought about how she'd put it, perhaps:

"With most men, a woman has to struggle to be beautiful and desirable in order to hold him. Not Milo, P." (She had taken to calling him simply P.) "With Milo, it's quite the contrary. I *do* believe that if I were to announce tomorrow that I was going on a ten-day salt-free reducing diet to improve my shape, he'd feel as miserable as another man would feel if his wife were to announce she was going to pick her teeth at a very social sit-down dinner party."

Rubbing herself with a turkish towel as she climbed from the tub, Gloria Wealdon wondered if P. was in love with her. He had never said so right out like that, but neither had he ever said he was in love with anyone else. He laughed quite a lot when they were together, and one evening at the Oak Bar in the Plaza Hotel he had said quite spontaneously: "I care for you very much, Gloria. You *are* important to me."

When she put the talcum on her body, she remembered the way Milo always wanted to get her in on the bed after a bath. He always used to call her Glo at those times. There was something about Milo that made him drop the last half of a person's name if he was terribly passionate about them, or extremely sorry for them. The way he referred to his Rosary Peas as his Rosas that fall they died on him because their pot was not big enough for their roots. My poor Rosas, he had said, my little Rosas…. And Glo, when he wanted to get her in on the bed. Dacky

Kent, his friend who had been studying to be a priest, was Dack after he died, and the good Lord only knows why Milo had one day called that mousey little salesclerk, Miss Dare, Edwin. Gloria remembered that she and Milo had come across Edwina Dare at the railroad station, where Milo had driven to pick up some punching bags he had had shipped from Cleveland which were to be installed in the high school gymnasium. They had stopped just for a second or so, both to say they were sorry Miss Dare was moving away from Cayuta, and hoping she would like it in Michigan (though heaven knew Gloria did not care a hoot). Out of a clear blue sky it had come — Milo's voice saying, "Well, Edwin, goodbye now."

She had even teased him about it on the way home. "Have you been fooling around with Edwina Dare or something? All of a sudden she's Edwin."

"I liked her," he had said.

"That would figure," Gloria had told him. "Just give you one unattractive, old maid spinster nobody gives a good goddamn about, and you're all set to play Prince Charming."

When she had finished dressing, Gloria stood before the full-length mirror in her navy blue suit with the saffron scarf tied at her neck. In her hand she carried the beige suede gloves and the navy bucket bag. She was no beauty, she realized that, but for once she felt that she had at last acquired good taste. Thanks to Pitts.

"Never be obvious," he had instructed her. "If you're wearing a navy blue suit, avoid white at the neck and white gloves to match. It's too much like a Polish maid's Easter Sunday in Ida Grove, Iowa. Whatever color you wear at your neck, never let it match exactly your glove color."

After she had bought the full-length mink, Pitts had said, "Very well, I suppose you *had* to buy mink. But remember, a lady never wears mink before five in the afternoon, or wool after five."

She had returned the mink the following day.

Gloria thought of the way Fern Fulton flounced about Cayuta at high noon in her mink, and she decided that the next time she and Fern had a little talk, she would mention the matter. If Freddy was so concerned with the rules of decorum, he would do well to teach them to that cross-eyed hoyden of theirs.

Just as Fern had been about to pour their second cups of coffee that morning, Virginia had appeared and undertaken the task. At least three times Gloria had said *one* teaspoon of sugar. Yet when the monster handed her the cup, the coffee was saturated with it. Gloria had been barely able to finish it, and the only reason she had was to pacify Fern. More and more toward the end of their visit, Fern seemed on the brink of overt rage.

Walking through the living room, Gloria found Milo standing by the table, flipping through Stanley's manuscript. He was just about to pop a coconut ice into his mouth.

"Sweets for the sweet, Milo?" she said. She knew how he disliked being caught eating candy. Milo was always off on tirades about the way sweets made cavities.

She said, "What on earth are you hanging around for? I thought you had to leave!"

Her husband shoved the candy and tissue into his pocket. "You could drop me off," he said. "On the way I'll stop in Stewart Drugs for you and get your anti-acid prescription filled." He held out his hand, the red pill wiggling in the palm. "This is your last one. You'll need some for tonight."

After every meal she had to swallow one of the pills, to get through her next few hours comfortably.

Milo liked to remind her of the fact, to point up his own iron constitution. She took the pill and slipped it into her change purse.

"I can get my own prescription filled."

"I wasn't sure you'd want to face Louie Stewart," he said. "After all, you practically called him an out-and-out pansy in your book."

"Did you forget that I'm having lunch with Louie's mother, Milo?"

"I doubt that Louie's forgiven you, even if Min has. And I doubt that Min has."

"I don't care … either way."

"One day," Milo said, "you're not going to land on your feet."

"Are you looking forward to picking up my broken bones from the ground, darling? The great big prince rescuing the little bitsy Cinderella?"

Milo turned his back to her and lit a cigarette. "I suppose your literary agent is the great lover?"

"Why don't you ask him at dinner tonight? Oh, Lord! That reminds me. I've got to remember the name of that wine Pitts likes. It's a rosy wine."

"Rose-zay," said Milo. "I won't be at dinner."

"Working late with the parallel bars and rope trapezes? Or is there an important conference at the ping-pong table?"

Milo told her to shut up. He whispered it.

"Why don't you ask that new teacher with the piano legs to go on a hundred-yard dash with you under the stars, Milo? Or you could pole vault by the light of the moon."

Milo took the car keys from his pocket. He turned back and faced his wife. "We better be going," he said sourly, "or you'll be late for your appointment…. Catch!" he called, tossing the keys with his infallible aim. They hit her across the bridge of the nose.

"Whoops! Sorry, Glor." He picked them off the floor and handed them to her.

She looked at him, rubbing the tip of her suede glove along her nosebone, her eyes watery from the stinging blow.

"Now do you feel better, Milo?"

He did indeed. His headache was gone.

Eight

> *Dr. Hammerheim was the local Freud; and it was not always a case of mispronunciation when some citizens referred to him as the local fraud.*
> — FROM *Population 12,360*

That afternoon while he was waiting for the light on Court Street, Jay Mannerheim noticed the car in front of him. Gloria Wealdon was driving, with Milo slumped beside her in the front seat. As the light went green and Jay turned at the corner, he began to think about the furor Gloria's novel had created in Cayuta.

It had served to remind him of the fact that the human ego was pitifully fragile, grievously vulnerable; that human beings were far more complex and peculiar than they were already assumed to be.

For instance, there was Freddy Fulton's family.

There was Fern, poor, lonely soul. At one time, probably back in the beginning of her analysis, she had told Gloria Wealdon the delicious falsehood that she and Jay were having an affair. It was innocent enough, as a fantasy *(some* of Jay's patients murdered him in *theirs)* and it was common enough among his female patients. But when Gloria had written it into her novel, Fern felt ruined in Jay's eyes.

When the book was first published, she spent most of

her analytic hour talking about it.

"I suppose," she would begin, "that you imagine I told Gloria a lie about us. It would be a ridiculous lie for me to tell," she would continue, "because I don't have to make up stories about my attractiveness. Why, I used to fight the boys off, down at Laura Bryan's dancing school, when I was a girl. One boy — he's a big man in stocks and bonds now and lives in Fairfield County — broke his collarbone racing across to dance with me. Jack Fowler was his name. Fowler and Nash, ever hear of them? Stocks and bonds."

Then she would reach suddenly for the Kleenex box on Jay's desk, and start to cry.

Sometimes she cried the whole fifty minutes, just sat and cried.

Once she said, "I think everyone in town is laughing at me because of that book. I think they all believe I told Gloria Wealdon we were having an affair! I never did, you know. *You* don't think I did, do you?"

"What do you think I think?" Jay had answered.

"You laugh at me too," she said.

That was untrue. Jay Mannerheim realized an immense pity for Freddy Fulton's wife. She had an almost sticky hunger for love, so that being in her presence was like walking through a too-humid hot August afternoon, when you felt as though you were powerless to accomplish anything at all. Sometimes Jay felt that all he could do for her was simply to listen, simply to take her money so she could buy those moments in his presence when there was no more façade, when there was just this miserable woman face-to-face with herself, looking into a mirror where there was reflected the shabby soap-opera of a lifetime; looking at truth instead of for it, the way someone will when dreams are over.

Now, with Gloria Wealdon's book published, it was as though everyone else could look too; look and point and make fun. Fern Fulton might have been able to convince Gloria Wealdon that she and Jay were having an affair, but most everyone else suspected the truth. Even Freddy Fulton had laughed at the idea. Freddy had said he wished Jay *would* have an affair with her.

Fulton puzzled Jay Mannerheim. From all he could gather, Freddy was never unfaithful to his wife, yet Fern confessed that up until about eight months ago their sexual activity had been only spasmodic for some six years. Now it was resuming with surprising frequency. Mannerheim supposed Fulton had either been neurotic in some unknown area, or guilty about whatever he imagined was *his* contribution to their child's eye condition. The latter, most probably. Many times people displaced guilt and punished another by withholding love. Still, how had Fulton overcome it, and had the novel Gloria Wealdon wrote had something to do with it? It seemed unlikely. Fulton was too sharp a man for such a glib likelihood; at the same time, he always seemed so easy-going and content, not like someone wrestling with some inner conflict so sexual in its nature. Jay could always see him in his mind's eye laughing with his head thrown back, standing that way he did with his legs apart, rocking on his heels, his slight paunch poking out in front of him, holding a drink with the ice melting in it (because he wasn't a fast drinker). Freddy Fulton, philosophical in a sort of kind and cynical way (like a much older man who'd known great love, passion or some kind of adventure). A nice guy, laughing, grinning, winking, saying something too wise and quite clever. He was very much like Milo Wealdon, in a stronger way; Milo was a weak sister to a Freddy Fulton, yet in both there was some uncanny spark, a look in the eye, a spring in the walk, something different that made you like them for a reason you couldn't honestly fathom. You just liked them, that was all.

Fern Fulton had said in her last session, "I wish Freddy would think we were having an affair! If there were only some way I could make him believe it!"

"Why do you want him to believe that?" Jay had said, even though he knew the answer, even though for her sake he, too, almost wished Freddy Fulton wouldn't laugh it off.

Then, there was Virginia Fulton's telephone call yesterday afternoon:

"I'd like to come and see you, Doctor."

"Well, Virginia, how are you?"

"Did you know Gloria Wealdon is back in town?"

"Is she?"

"I'd like to come and see you on business."

"I wouldn't worry about Gloria Wealdon, Virginia." He supposed Fern had been making the same threats at home as she did during her analytic hour. He added, "She can take care of herself, don't you think?" chuckling.

"Perhaps."

"How have you been, Virginia?"

"All right."

"And your dad?"

"He's fine."

"Gloria Wealdon can take care of herself, honey."

"I'm sorry if I bothered you…. It was just — "

"You didn't bother me at all. In fact, I'm just about ready to go and play some golf, get the kinks out."

"Yes," said Virginia Fulton. "Well, goodbye."

But it was not Freddy Fulton's family alone who were affected by the novel. Jay could think of others, and that noon he thought of two in particular. One person was Roberta Shagland from the high school. *She* was attempting to cope with an altogether different sort of threat —

the threat of an intense attraction to Milo Wealdon. It
had come over her while she was reading his wife's book.

"I just feel so sorry for him, Doctor," she had told Jay.
"I know that woman is mean to him, mean as anything!
Every time I think of it, I just hate her! I can't concentrate
on another thing but him, do you know? I mean, I'd like
to make him feel wanted, do you know? Then I start this
hiccuping I was telling you about. Doctor, I get hiccups."
She was always twisting a wet hanky in her hand during
her hour. "I don't know what I'm going to do."

"I don't think it's so serious," said Jay. "I don't think
we have to worry a lot about it."

"But what can I do to stop it?"

"We'll work it out."

"I'm just so pent up, do you know? I even dream about
him."

"I know."

"And I feel like crying all the time, Doctor."

Miss Shagland was Mannerheim's newest patient. She
had begun her consultations (the doctor was convinced
that was all they would amount to, that she would hardly
need continual treatment) immediately after reading *Population 12,360*. There was another who had done the
same, though he had started a week or two before Miss
Shagland. He was the second person Jay Mannerheim
thought of — Louie Stewart.

Louie did not cry, and he refused to stretch out on the
couch. He sat soldier-straight in the armless, leather high-
back chair, opposite Jay's desk, and pared his nails with a
squeaky silver clip. At some sessions, Louie said very little.
After long silences, he would announce in flat, deep, stac-
cato: "Hate!"

"Hate who?" Jay would say.

Louie's answers varied.

"I am not as quixotic as you may think," he said once,
ignoring Jay's question. "I have hidden, vitriolic potential!"

Another time, he said, "It's a huge joke!"

"What is?"

"A surreptitious undertaking of mine, which I am not at liberty to think about fully at this time."

When he was voluble, he concentrated on the mechanical and grammatical errors in Gloria Wealdon's novel.

"On page 232," he would say, "there is a typo! Words run together!" His face would get very flushed, and he would lean forward in his chair and crack his knuckles, gripping his hands together so tightly the knuckles went white. He would complain that the pronouns and antecedents in the novel did not agree, that prefixes were not solid with their stems, that there were infinite bromides and redundancies.

"Aren't you dwelling too much on the book itself?" Jay would ask him. "What's really bothering you, Louie? What she wrote about some character in the book?" Silence ... then: "Do you think you're in the book, Louie? Is that it?"

Louie would give no indication he had heard the questions.

"She said 'feeling ran high' eighteen times," he would answer. "Eighteen times!"

Jay Mannerheim was deeply concerned about Louie Stewart. The boy (and no one in Cayuta ever thought of him as a young man, though he was well into his thirties) had always been mixed-up and sissyfied. But now, it was quite another story. Jay was pretty certain that Min Stewart's son was not even a neurotic, but a full-blown certifiable psychotic. This afternoon, during Louie's session, Jay was going to decide whether to continue treatment or to recommend to Min that Louie be examined by the physicians at the Cayuta Retreat.

The credit was not Gloria Wealdon's for all of this, not by any means. In all cases, she simply touched off some-

THE GIRL ON THE BEST SELLER LIST

thing that would have gone off sooner or later anyway; she was the catalyst. But the less serious irritations, the minor embarrassments many in Cayuta had suffered since the publication of *Population 12,360* she *could* take credit for. For her portrayal of Virginia Fulton, for that of her hero, Milo, for the thinly disguised characterization of Min Stewart. For these, the blame rested fully on her, and for some others, probably — smaller ones, where there was only a sting instead of a full punch to the stomach. She had made war on Cayuta, New York, and there was no doubt that there were battle scars and casualties, no doubt either that there would be law suits. Out of it all, Jay felt mostly sorry for Milo Wealdon; yet again, why was that thought always followed by the thought that probably Milo did not need his sympathy? It was an enigma.

Jay himself had minded only one thing about Gloria Wealdon's portrayal of him, and that was her emphasis on the fact that he was not a medical doctor. It had angered him, in fact. All of his patients understood that he was a psychologist and not a psychoanalyst, and in the county he really had no competition. So his anger was not inspired out of any feeling that she had exposed him, or driven potential patients to an M.D. in the same area. It was rooted primarily in two sentences of conversation in the novel, when two women were discussing entering analysis:

> "*Don't go to Dr. Hammerheim,*" *said Gina to Fernanda,* "*if you have to get psychoanalyzed. Go to a real doctor, an M.D. Then you can take it off your income tax as a medical expense, but you can't do it unless you go to a real doctor.*"
>
> "*I suppose you're right,*" *Fernanda exclaimed.* "*Why, I'd never thought of that!*"

Neither had a good many people in Cayuta thought of that, Mannerheim knew; neither had the local tax inspectors. It had probably never occurred to them to notice this very technical but terribly damaging fact. Jay was a perfectly legitimate psychologist, but the tax exemption rules could not be clearer. Only last week at Tuesday's Rotary, Bill Farley, one of the county government men, said, "That's a Ph.D. you've got, eh, Mannerheim."

"Yes," Jay had said. "Why?"

"I just got to get all these D's straight," Farley'd smiled. "Ph.D., M.D. — just try to sort them out."

"Sure," Jay had said. "That's your job."

"'At's right." Farley'd clapped him across the back, chewing his half-smoked cigar. Then, unnecessarily, he'd added: "I got nothin' against either, mind you. It's just that I gotta keep 'em straight."

Remembering it, Jay shrugged. She was a bitch, all right, he thought, boy she was a bitch! He turned west on Genesee Street, and as he did he spotted Stanley Secora idling on the corner. It reminded him that the front windows of his office needed cleaning, and he slowed to call the boy over to the car. Even Secora was not unaffected by Gloria Wealdon's novel, Jay mused, as he waved at the young fellow, though how Stanley Secora managed to squeeze himself into the confusion, Jay couldn't figure out. He supposed Secora just had a good case of celebrity worship. The last time he had done the windows for Jay, her picture, cut from a newspaper, had fallen out of his trousers' pocket as he had reached there for a rag to wipe dry the panes.

Nine

*He taught school, but whatever he inspired in
his students was a mystery, save for Gina's guess
that he might inspire all of them to want to be
anything in this life but a teacher....*
Who would want to be like Miles?
— FROM *Population 12,360*

After he had been dropped off at the high school by his
wife, Milo stopped by the tennis courts to watch little
Mickey Lewis practice for the term play-offs. A few of his
students were also watching, a scattering of them on the
white benches behind the high rails. He waved at them
and then thought what he was always thinking lately —
they were talking about him. He had an idea that what
they said was favorable.

He knew there were jokes around about Gloria's book,
and he knew that a few of his pupils even called him
Miles behind his back, but he also knew that for the most
part everyone wondered why he stayed with Gloria, why
he didn't divorce her because of the book. He knew he
was well-liked, but he knew lots of the boys in his classes
wanted to ask him the same question Mickey Lewis had
asked him last week:

"Mr. Wealdon, sir, why don't you divorce her?"

It had just popped out of Mickey's mouth, and his quick
gesture of clamping his palm across his lips had not saved
the moment for Mickey.

"She's my wife," Milo had answered. "You know,
Mickey, it's a little like a ball team, a marriage is — smaller,
but still a team. A good team sticks together, even when
someone on it doesn't do right by the team. You have to
have a lot of patience and understanding. Remember a

couple of days ago when we were talking about Ken Boyer with the Cardinals?"

"I remember," said Mickey. "They almost traded him in '58."

"That's right, and now it looks like he's going to be the same kind of heavy-handed slugger that started with Rogers Hornsby and went from there to Bottomley, to Medwick, to Mize — "

"Right up to Musial," said Mickey. "I suppose I get your point. I'm sorry I said it."

"Don't be sorry, Mickey," Milo had said. "Just keep in mind that responsibility toward the members of a team can sometimes make that team, when nothing else can."

Milo knew that if Gloria had been witness to his comparison of her with a third-baseman for the St. Louis Cardinals, she would have burst with that particular brand of Gloria Wealdon mocking hilarity. Yet a sense of responsibility was instinctive to Milo, no matter how poorly he had put it to Mickey Lewis. Whether or not Gloria could pay her own way now (and she could), so long as she was alive he was obliged to care for her. To care about her. The fact that some people thought him an utter ass to persist in this under the circumstances did not deter him. He felt no need to defend his philosophy of life beyond explaining it. The only thing that really annoyed him about his situation was the surreptitious pettiness sneaking up on him and showing in his own actions. The satisfaction he had gotten from hitting her with the car keys a while ago, his sarcasm as he had slammed the door of the car. (He had said, Remember your stomach pill, pet....) There was no need for that. She would have taken the pill and that would be that; there was no need for the remark. It was small, piddling. His reactions to her lately were very much like hers to him, and he was embarrassed for himself.

He very nearly decided to go home for dinner in the evening, to go home and change his clothes and play the proper husband — meet this literary agent of Gloria's and serve as host for the dinner she had planned. Perhaps, under the circumstances, it was the least he could do. Yet if he were to change his plans, he would have to alter his course of action, and he had planned that for too long, put it off too often. He must see his plot through in every detail, or it might not work.

At the end of Mickey's set, Milo walked over to the fence where the youngster was picking a hand towel up off the ground to rub away his perspiration. Mickey was nearly sixteen, but he was barely five feet tall and Milo had known him since he was a kid of ten, when Mickey hung around the Y courts, eager to learn about tennis. Because he was so small, Milo had taught him a two-forehand technique which would give him more power and more reach, and by the time Mickey entered high school he still did not use a backhand. Milo never tried to make him learn it. The youngster was naturally ambidextrous. He wrote left-handed, and threw a ball right-handed, and in the back court during a game he switched his racket from one hand to the other so swiftly and easily that the lack of a backhand went hardly noticed.

Mickey grinned at Milo. "How'm I doing, Mr. Wealdon?"

"You're doing okay, Mickey. Those were good hard hits from the base line."

"There's still something wrong though, huh?"

"You know it as well as I do. You have to charge that net and volley, Mickey."

"I know."

"You can do your racket-shifting just as well close. You try it. You'll need it for your doubles game."

"Yessir. I know that. I like my opponents to take over the net, but it's a bad habit. Say, want to volley with me,

Mr. Wealdon? You can use Dave's racket?"

"Right!" Milo said.

After twenty minutes of play, Milo returned the racket to Dave Pompton. Pompton was a huge fellow, Mickey Lewis's age, with muscles that were short and bunchy like a weightlifter's or a furniture mover's.

He was a good baseball player, with ambitions to become a professional, but with all the quick stops and starts in the game, he was always pulling and tearing the muscles. Milo had gotten him to take up swimming for his arm and leg muscles, pushups for his back, and tennis to coordinate everything.

"How's everything coming now?" said Milo.

"I think I'm getting there. I feel loose, no kidding."

"You'll be fine, Dave. You know Moose Skowron had your trouble."

Dave Pompton laughed. "You mean *I* had *his* trouble, don't you?"

"You'll be better than Moose if you hit the way you did last Monday!"

"Thanks, Mr. Wealdon," Mickey Lewis called as Milo walked away from the inside of the court.

Dave's thanks echoed Mickey's. Then before the pair resumed their game, Milo heard Mickey say, "He ought to have kids."

"With *her*?" was Dave's answer.

Milo went back by the benches and continued to watch Mickey. He watched him charge the net a few times, and saw him handle the racket shift adequately. He watched Dave's muscles flex as he reached for the high balls, and while he watched, he kept hearing the last words Dave had spoken: With *her*? Like a broken record: With *her*? With *her*? Her?

He wished, in some ways, that Gloria had consented to

have a child with him. He knew all the psychologists and moralists and arm-chair philosophers claimed a child needed the love of both parents, parents who were in love; but when he thought of Freddy Fulton and his daughter, he wished he had a son or a daughter himself. In many ways, Freddy's kid was more similar to Edwina Dare in her personality than she was to Fern. Virginia was bright and shy and retiring, and probably never going to be very pretty — but she *was* real. Milo supposed it was particularly unkind of him even to have the thought that Freddy's daughter was like Freddy's ex-love. (Ex? No, that was just a convenient way of stating the fact she was no longer visible in Freddy's life, but she would always be there, Milo guessed.) But Milo often wished he had even that much, some human reminder that his personality had been integrated into something more than soap sculptures, or shrubbery, or kids that came back after they'd been graduated from college and said, Do you remember me, Mr. Wealdon? and shook his hand and were glad to see him again.

Gloria had always said very bluntly, "I wouldn't be a fit mother, Milo. I hate children," and he could hardly disagree with her about the impracticality of their having any. But he quite often mourned the missed opportunity, and though he was not one to really brood over past mistakes, occasionally, when he reflected on his own shortcomings, he was sorry that he had never discouraged that trait in him which was responsible for his having confused love and pity to such an extent.

He had read somewhere that love and hate had the same opposite — indifference. He had never been able to be indifferent to Gloria, not from the first moment he had seen her standing alone in that crowd at Cornell, looking sullen and sadly neglected. He supposed that what he felt even now, whenever someone laughed at her or showed her up, or even thought of him as a fool to stand by her — whatever made him still want to shield her, made him feel the inner twinge of anger at others' abuse of her — must no longer have to do with his love for her; rather, now, it had to do with his hatred for her. Because the fact remained, he was not indifferent to Gloria.

He was standing there pondering this when Roberta Shagland drove up in her tiny Volkswagen. It was an old model, not a convertible, and Milo didn't know why he felt sorry about *that,* but he did. She looked all the more large (though she was really not a big woman) as she got out of the car, and because she got out legs first, what Milo saw first were her gigantic ankles. He turned away, not to avoid her, but to make her think he did not see her in that situation. As he turned away he was aware that his gesture, intended as kindliness toward her, was horribly unkind, and he was glad that it was impossible for people to know others' thoughts. Even Gloria had sensed something about him — a detestable something that had warranted her remark this morning: "You married me because *I* was a creep, or didn't you think I'd figured that out?" It had stunned him slightly when she had said it. It had made him feel quite ill in his stomach. How had the act of love come to be interpreted in so many ways nowadays; how had its manifestations come to be all sorted out and classified in ugly vials and labeled so that now love was almost a danger, a trap, a way of exposing your most horribly personal inner self.

Milo remembered something that had happened once about a year ago. It was while he was reading in the Chronicle of the Abbey of Fontevrault, just after he had made his sculpture of St. Augustine. It was a story about the death of a nun who had after death appeared to one of her sisters in religion, saying, "Understand, my love, that I am already in great peace; but I do not know how to enter paradise without you. Therefore come quickly so that we may go in together."

Milo had made the mistake of sharing with Gloria his pleasure in this passage. When he had finished reading it to her, she had let out a hoot of laughter. "You see?" she had said.

"What's funny?"

"It's all so much crap, Milo! They're a couple of goddam lesbians."

"Of course," he had said sourly, closing the book. "Of course."

"Those saints and all those holy characters were sick, sick, sick!" she laughed. "Jesus! What if I ever wrote a letter like that to Fern Fulton? Do you know what people would say?"

"No," Milo said tiredly, on his way to his room now.

"That I was queer," said Gloria after him, "and you *know* it!"

There was no more, it seemed, the simple act of loving without caring why. There was all the fallout from Freud, filtering down on all peoples.

Behind him Roberta Shagland said, "What are you doing here on a Saturday, Coach?"

Everyone knew that Milo was at the school every Saturday. Milo knew, too, that she was here for the meeting with the school board, about the change in menu for the cafeteria.

He said, "I'm here every Saturday."

"All work and no play," she laughed.

He laughed too, but too generously. He said, "But what brings you here?"

"The school board," she said. "We're going to discuss a change in menu for the cafeteria."

"Oh?" He acted surprised.

"Well, we could use a change."

"Yes."

"Yes."

"Who's the tennis champ, Coach?"

He didn't like her to call him Coach. He would never tell her that, but it seemed too nicely to indicate an authority that was not valid. "The young Lewis boy is pretty good," he said.

"Do you play, Coach?"

"Not tennis. I was never very good at it."

That was an untruth. At Cornell he had been very good at every sport, but most successful at team sports, or solo sports like skiing. At competitive sports that involved two players, Milo had the unsportsman-like tendency to let the other fellow win, for no reason. He remembered that whenever, during a game of tennis, it was his part to call across the net, "Take two," he felt like adding, "or three, or as many as you like." He was good at it, but tennis was not his game.

Roberta Shagland said, "I love the game."

He could not help it that it came to his mind: a picture of her in a white tennis skirt, then beneath the skirt the white sneakers, and above the sneakers — those ankles! He wanted to make it up to her that he had had that thought. He said, "You look very nice today."

The change in subject seemed to fluster her. She blushed.

He said, "I don't think it will rain, either."

It was preposterous to have said that. It made her all the more confused.

He said, "I mean, for my track meet."

"Oh, I know you meant that," she hastened to say. "I know what you meant."

He said, "Perhaps you'll come to the meet." There it was — the invitation.

Roberta Shagland hiccupped. "Excuse me."

"That's all right."

"Yes, I'd like to see a meet." A hiccup. "I never have." Another.

"You ought to have a glass of water," he said.

"I'm going inside now."

"Drink it very slowly," he said. "That usually does the trick."

It was such banal repartee. He felt so sorry for her, and somehow responsible for her hiccups. He was more embarrassed by them, he was certain, than she was.

But it was she who fled.

She said, "I'll see you later."

He looked after her and felt a little sad. He wished he had been somewhere where he could have gotten her the glass of water.

He watched the tennis players a little longer. He began to feel more relaxed, not as depressed as before. With the lessening of anxiety, came determination; tonight he would carry it out. He wouldn't postpone it any longer, he was sure of that. Even though he was sorry for Gloria, even though he had an obligation, so long as she lived, to care for and about her, his plot would deliver him…. Revenge? That was a strange word in the light of what he was planning to do, but it was also strange, he decided, that love and hate should have the same opposite. A lot of things were strange in life, and, as he turned away from the tennis court and walked toward the school, Milo decided that not the least of these was the word "love" in a tennis game. It meant zero….

Ten

If Stewie had any backbone, he would probably have been arrested half a dozen times already for indecent acts, but his record was as lily-clean as his long hands always were, and he was too dull to be a menace, so he was an embarrassing bore. Women didn't even feel inclined to mother him, as often happens with Stewies in life; and men, of

course, were nervous around him because he was
silly and never immoral, so that they could not
punch him in the nose, or report him, or even ex-
claim, "Goddam fairy!", because he really wasn't
anything anyone could cuss away in a few words;
he was just that suspicious species of male which
hangs in Limbo, like an unspoken threat.
      — FROM *Population 12,360*

Louie Stewart liked it best back in the prescription department of the drug store his mother owned. There it
was quiet and Louie could think constructively. But before
he went there, it was necessary to sit at the soda fountain,
order a lemon Coke, and decide which Thought he would
choose. Louie had a "thought system," to avoid random
thinking, which was wasteful. And Louie detested waste.
He worshipped order.
   One of the things that drew him back to the prescription
department even more than the quiet was the unique at-
mosphere of perfection. Louie loved the rows of bottles,
the motley pills — each one counted, each one assigned,
all in their places. He believed evil stemmed from disorder,
and one of the reasons he *chose* his thoughts each day
was so that he could organize his mind, and keep it from
straying toward wickedness.
   That noon as he poked the straw down between the ice
cubes in the glass, he was experiencing the same confusion
which had been plaguing him for weeks. His thinking ran
ahead of him like a wild and unruly child, and he found
himself dwelling on Gloria Wealdon's novel. It was very
nearly an obsession with him now. He kept it hidden behind the pill bottles, the way someone would hide contra-
band. Already the pages had the slackness of a well-pe-
rused reference book; the cover was torn from constant
handling, and when Louie was searching for a certain
part in the novel, he was able to find it in seconds.

Louie was long like a big skinny spider, with red hair and the inevitable freckles splashed across his countenance. He was thirty-five. When he was a child, arithmetic had been his hobby, and as he grew, he had expanded it to algebra, geometry, trigonometry, and ultimately, calculus. His ambition, at thirteen, had been to be an accountant, but when he had told his mother, she only nodded and went right on sipping her sweet vermouth aperitif and turned a page of her Henry James novel. He felt ashamed for having said it, and he took it back instantly: "I was kidding. Don't you know when I'm kidding, Mums?" Then she smiled, put her book on her lap, and they talked about what his day had been like.

After that, he changed his ambition to a Thought; he listed it along with the others as: The Thought of Being an Accountant.

When he chose it, he imagined himself bent over the huge ledgers with their long-lined yellow paper, and the neat rows of figures under Losses, Gains, Leakages, and Economies. He enjoyed this Thought a great deal; he saved it for special days, believing that if he indulged himself too often it would be spoiled.

Still, he admitted that his mother had been right. He was much better off working in the drug store. One day he would be sole owner, and when he was, he would put into practice some of his own ideas. One he had devised was for doctors' prescription pads. Their handwriting was so consistently wretched that Louie had worked out a system for pads with the prescriptions already printed upon them. The doctor need only sign his illegible name. It was a deliciously complicated system because of the variety in prescriptions and, in addition, Louie had devised a number system, along with a letter system, which encompassed the most common formulas, as well as directions for their use, such as *one a day, two before meals,* or *take when drowsy.*

With Louie dispensing these pads to the doctors, it would mean more business, since they could only be used at Stewart Drugs. It was a grand and practical idea, and while Louie wished his dear (vital!) mother no harm, it was annoying to have to wait for the day when he could put it into effect. Meanwhile, he said nothing about it to her, for fear of ridicule. He kept it as one of his Thoughts.

Louie's mother was usually right about what was good for Louie. He would be the first to say so, and he would add to it that his mother was usually right about what was good for most people. She had saved the Fultons' marriage back in 1953, hadn't she? Louie had been only twenty-six then, but he still remembered hanging over the banister upstairs, dressed in his pajamas, listening on those nights his mother had "talks" downstairs with Freddy Fulton.

"But I love her, Min," he remembered Fulton saying. "I am truly very deeply in love with Edwina."

"You're romantically in love."

"Of course."

"Romantic love is the worst kind, Frederick. It's ephemeral."

"Not ours."

"No, no one ever thinks *his* is, but take my word for it. Frederick, you have the child to think about."

"I know."

"And your wife as well."

"The only thing that makes me hesitate, that makes me ask for your advice, Min, is my daughter. She'll need me. I can't imagine Fern raising her properly or giving her any kind of happiness."

"Your daughter will need you both, Frederick. Edwina Dare doesn't *need* you."

"She loves me."

"Frederick, romantic love thrives on obstruction; it's the only kind of love that does. You complained earlier that your business is failing. It is not your business, it's your integrity. Regardless of how well-kept your secret has been in Cayuta, your emotional involvement is showing. You lost the Lindgren account because you weren't on your toes. I suppose that's the reason the bank refused your loan."

"I love her, Min."

"How much? Enough to give up your daughter and your firm? To break your wife's heart and spirit? And you know I've always admired Fern's spirit. I hope your daughter inherits some of it."

"I've never thought of Fern as having spirit."

"Confusion doesn't scare her, Frederick, even when it's her own inner confusion. She speaks it out, acts it out. I suppose it seems too obvious a way for you, but I like it. Sometimes subtlety is merely a façade to pretense."

"I want to thank you, Min, no matter how I decide."

"And should you decide to abandon your Edwina, Frederick, I'll advance you the capital the bank refused."

Louie still remembered it all — how his mother had placidly piloted Fulton's moods from rage to agonized whimpering to self-pity to ultimate resigned acceptance of her advice, advice which was really more of a proposition. There were three conditions attached to her loan: that Fern Fulton was not to know he had been persuaded by her to keep his marriage intact, that he was to convince Edwina Dare to leave Cayuta, and that for the period it took Fulton to repay the loan, the products of his pharmaceutical supply company were to be sold to Stewart Drugs at cost.

After Louie finished his lemon Coke, still without having chosen his Thought, he ordered another. He tried not to, because it was not part of his ritual to have two, but his anxiety about everything lately made him relent. If only he could get it across to Doctor Mannerheim that what he hated about that novel, was that there were errors all through it, misspellings and misprints and words running together! He got a grip on himself after he felt his hands squeeze the glass too hard; his teeth began their grinding, and he thought, easy now, fellow, eeee-zee! In his mind he pictured a mathematical formula.

Then he felt better. It was a way he had of bringing himself under control — by factoring.

The soda jerk handed him his second lemon Coke, and Louie spun around on the red leather chair and faced the door. When he saw the woman coming into the drug store, Louie's mind began to whirl. He held tight to the glass and fought desperately for control.

After Gloria Wealdon left Stewart Drugs that noon, with the anti-acid prescription Louie had filled for her, she put her car in the lot behind the Cayuta Hotel. She went inside through the restaurant entrance.

At a side corner table, Min Stewart was waiting for her.

As Gloria crossed the thick saffron carpet, she felt suddenly sure that her stocking seams were crooked. She was conscious of the hangnail on her thumb, and aware of the fact that even though she had dressed carefully, following all the rules Pitts had set forth, she was somehow slovenly.

She did not mean to say, "Hi! How's it go?" It just happened, vulgar-sounding and hicky.

Min was sipping a vermouth cassis. She nodded and smiled thinly.

Gloria had tried to fix her features in a disdainful, superior pose, but as she sat down, she glanced at her reflection in the mirror behind Min. She looked like someone with a stiff neck, who had just bitten into a bar of soap.

"A Martini," Gloria told the waiter. "Dry, with a lemon peel. How are you, Mrs. Stewart? You wanted to see me about something?"

Min Stewart managed another wry smile. "There is no

necessity to discuss it immediately. How was your New York visit?"

Another rush of ill-chosen words escaped from Gloria Wealdon: "I think you ought to get it off your chest right off the bat."

"Very well, then." Min Stewart patted her silver hair, touched a long, manicured finger to the pearl choker at her neck, and brought the finger down to rest on the sleeve of her soft, brown wool suit. "I would like to talk about my son."

"I just spoke to Louie a moment ago, in the drug store."

The remark went unacknowledged. That fact made heat rise to Gloria Wealdon's neck. What was it about a person like Min Stewart that gave her the right to be so pompous? Why was Gloria Wealdon always in the position of playing the fly to her spider.

Min Stewart, pausing to sip her drink, said, "He's under doctor's care."

"He looks good."

"Yes, Louie does look *well*. But he doesn't feel well. Doctor Mannerheim is treating him."

"Oh?" Gloria smiled wryly. "*That* kind of doctor."

She imagined that the idea of a psychoanalyst treating a Stewart, from Min Stewart's viewpoint, was synonymous with a Rosicrucian's converting Princess Margaret.

Except for a slight tightening of the lips, Min Stewart was oblivious to any innuendo. "Doctor Mannerheim," she said, "feels that your novel has upset Louie."

"That's the way the ball bounces," Gloria said. It seemed that her choice of words when she spoke to Min Stewart made her all the more the clumsy person Min thought she was.

"Is it?" said Min. "Jay feels that something in the novel triggered a neurosis in Louie. He isn't sure of the nature of the neurosis; he feels Louie isn't either. For my own part, I am not concerned with the nature of it, merely with its dismissal." Min took another sip of the vermouth and set down the tiny, long-stemmed glass.

She said, "Jay feels it will take some time for Louie's problem to be resolved. I disagree with him."

"What has this got to do with me?"

But Min continued: "I believe that psychoanalysis, as valuable as it is, in many instances too readily offers a crutch to people whose problems might be solved quite simply." She paused, and slipped off the suit coat from her shoulders. Gloria looked to see if there was a label in the lining. Of course, there was not.

In her novel, Gloria had written about this eccentricity of Min's. She had not ascribed it to Min, because Min did not figure in the story, nor was there any character with a personality similar to hers. Yet she had described a woman purchasing an Emeric Partos coat from Bergdorf Goodman and requesting that the labels be removed. Like Min, Gloria's character did not believe she should be a vehicle for advertising.

Gloria repeated: "What has this got to do with me?"

Min Stewart smiled the way someone would smile at a restless child. "'Adopt the pace of nature,'" she said in cryptic-sounding tone, "'Her secret is *patience.*' ... Do you know who wrote that, my dear?"

"I suppose Shakespeare," said Gloria.

"Emerson."

"I wouldn't know about him."

"It's from 'The Over-Soul,'" said Min.

The waiter brought Gloria's Martini, and there was a respite then while lunch was ordered.

Gloria's stomach ache had not left her. It irritated her that she should have this problem again upon her return to Cayuta. Throughout her New York stay, no matter the circumstance, she had not experienced a nervous stomach. She had thought the security she had felt with the publication of her novel had put an end to all that. Yet ever since her visit with Fern that morning the pain had been constant. In a way it was like those dreams she had had while she was writing her novel, dreams of being back at college and steeling herself for final examinations, frenzied nightmares of anxiety that she would fail all her subjects.

When the waiter left with their order, Min said, "My son has found innumerable errors in your novel, Mrs. Wealdon. I speak not of content but of such errors as those in editing, proofreading and typography. Simple, trivial errors, which Louie has listed, and which he persists in brooding over."

Gloria Wealdon took a gulp of her Martini. She was beginning to feel less unsure of herself now. She was pleased that she could think to say, "What am I supposed to do? Rewrite?"

"If you were to go to Louie," said Min, "and tell him that you feel that there were mistakes in the novel — that the printer and the editor had made mistakes — and if you were to ask him to point them out to you, I am confident that Louie would benefit greatly from the situation."

She looked into Gloria Wealdon's eyes carefully. "I do not say that Louie, when he *is* himself, is without peculiarity, but he functions. He has been unfortunate not to have had a father's guidance all his life. As a result, he is a little silly sometimes and a trifle absurd a good majority of the time. But he works hard. He's quite agreeable under normal circumstances."

Gloria remembered hearing that when Louie, Sr., had married Min, no one ever imagined he would continue at the drug store. Min was a Wadsworth girl with wealth of the best kind — inherited wealth. But Louis, Sr., was a stubborn individual. It was rumored that on his deathbed he gave two orders: "Let the dog sleep in the house nights now, Min, he's old" and "See that young Louie, when he grows up, carries on my business."

Gloria Wealdon said, "It was very important to me a few years back that I get into the Birthday Club. You kept me out, Mrs. Stewart. Do you remember?"

"I recall that your birthday is in January. We already have eight Januarys, and had that amount at the time your name came up."

"But now?"

Min's face was blank. "Now?"

"If I were to do this — favor, you would be willing to add to that amount." Gloria stated it as fact. Her lips tipped in a slight smile. She was impatient to refuse the invitation Min was obliged to extend.

"Eight is far too many already," said Min.

"Do you mean if I were to do what you ask, you'd still keep me out?"

"The idea behind the Birthday Club, Mrs. Wealdon, was to choose twelve women whose birthdays fell in the twelve months of the year. We had never intended to have more than twelve members. We have made far too many exceptions in the past, and we have decided unanimously that we won't make any more. So you see, it's out of my hands."

"And just what would I gain if I were to do what you ask?"

"Not a gain really, Mrs. Wealdon. It would be in the way of a saving."

"A saving?"

"Yes. You would save your life, I think."

"My life!" Gloria let out a hoot. Several people in the dining room turned to stare. Min Stewart's face was quiet and solemn.

"Are you kidding?" Gloria said.

"I very rarely *kid,* Mrs. Wealdon. This morning, my son was writing formulas on the tablecloth at breakfast. Quite often he does this when he's keenly distressed, but he never dirties anything. Louie is neat to a point where it is somewhat of a mania." She smiled. "I don't believe he realized what he was doing. I shouldn't like him to extend that mood to other areas, and I am not at all convinced that we — you — can afford to wait while Doctor Mannerheim attempts treatment. I know my son, Mrs. Wealdon. He is not a murderer, but I suspect he will kill you if too much time elapses before someone takes the necessary steps to prevent this."

"The police — "

"Yes, the police ... but they wouldn't believe you."

"And you wouldn't ...?"

"No, I wouldn't, Mrs. Wealdon."

"I've never heard of such a thing."

"'There are more things in heaven and earth, Horatio, than are dreamt of in your philosophy.'" Min Stewart finished the vermouth in her glass and added, "That *is* Shakespeare."

Gloria Wealdon tried to recall the details of her meeting with Louie Stewart, less than an hour ago.

The stomach ache persisted, seemed to grow. She tried to think. Was there anything out of the ordinary when she was in the drug store, any note of hostility from Louie, any remark, expression, anything at all like that? He had been most prompt in filling her prescription and most polite. There had been a minimum of palaver: Hello, how are you, yes, it is cool — no more, chit-chat was all. And Min Stewart was a fox, had always been one, had always gotten her way with everything and everyone. She would like Gloria Wealdon to make a fool of herself, to go to Louie that way, fearful of her life, crazy-acting and vulnerable to this hideously melodramatic chicanery. That was it, wasn't it?

"Ridiculous!" Gloria breathed. She could feel Min's eyes watching her.

She said aloud, "Simply ridiculous, the whole business."

Min Stewart looked beyond her toward the front of the restaurant. She said, matter-of-factly, "Since you brought up Shakespeare's writings, there was another saying attributed to him, Mrs. Wealdon. 'Don't take cannon-bullets for bird-bolts.'"

The waiter set a plate of osso buco at Gloria's place.

"Though I can't recall exactly *where* it is from," Min frowned. "Probably one of the minor tragedies."

Eleven

Fernanda raised her Rob Roy and clinked it against Gina's Martini. "Here's to that absolutely divine head-shrinker, the fabulous Dr. Hammerheim," she said.

"To Mr. Hammerheim," Gina corrected her. "Practicing phony!"

— FROM *Population 12,360*

Stanley Secora arrived at Jay Mannerheim's office ten minutes late. He knew the doctor's routine by now; he had often done odd jobs for him, and he knew how important it was to be punctual. His tardiness meant that Mannerheim was already with his one-thirty patient. Never under any circumstances, the doctor had always made clear, was he to be interrupted once a patient entered his office, and he shut the door leading down to the inner sanctum. There was a long hallway between the waiting room and the room where the doctor sat listening to whomever was on his couch. Stanley stood in the waiting room staring at the door to that hallway. On Saturdays the doctor had no help, so there was no one for Stanley to tell that he could not do as the doctor had asked. Stanley had known when Jay Mannerheim stopped him on Genesee Street at noon that he was in no condition to wash the doctor's windows. Still, he had said he would be there at one-twenty — he was *that* confused on this May day.

What had made him late was that he had tried to call Mrs. Wealdon, and, again, there was no answer. Ever since his meeting with her — that incredibly brief moment or two during which he had faced her in the Wealdon living room — he had been unable to keep from trembling. He had botched it badly, but she had not helped by hurrying him that way. He wanted to return; he *had* to return as soon as she got back. He planned to keep trying the number, then, when she answered, to hang up and go there. Yet part of him was afraid of this plan; part of him was already too wounded by the early encounter. Now that part tried to reason with him: What if she's not alone? Mr. Wealdon could be there by that time, or her agent, someone, anyone; and his trembling would mount with rage, and he would be at the same time furious and humiliated, like a bridegroom spurned on his wedding night.

There was another part of him, too, which wanted to tell Jay Mannerheim about it. He remembered an afternoon some months ago — he had been doing the doctor's windows — when the news clipping with Gloria Wealdon's picture had fallen from his pocket. He had felt very embarrassed for the doctor to see it. He had simply stood there blushing, with the picture on the floor between them. It was Jay Mannerheim who had bent down and handed it to him.

"Is this yours, Stanley." It had not been a question, just a remark.

Stanley had carelessly stuffed it back into his pants. "I admire her," he had said, "that's all."

"There's nothing wrong with that." Mannerheim was always so casual about everything.

"Did you read her book, Doctor?"

"Some of it."

Stanley wanted to ask him what he thought about those parts in which Will figured. He said instead, "I guess she wrote everybody up."

"I guess."

"You have to give her credit, don't you, Doctor?"

"Nobody else deserves the credit for it," Mannerheim said.

If he were to tell Mannerheim how he felt, he didn't think Mannerheim would laugh. Mannerheim never laughed at the things people said, and some of the things his patients said were very crazy. Stanley had heard them in there more than once. In the hallway between the waiting room and the doctor's office, you could hear very plainly anything that was going on. Stanley had done the windows there a couple of times when the doctor was practicing.

There was one afternoon when Stanley heard old Mrs. Highsmith yell, "I'm not crazy, you're making me crazy!"

Stanley had felt like guffawing, but he had managed to suppress his laughter and continue with his job.

Another time he had actually heard Mrs. Fulton in there. She had said, "He even takes her to Elbridge with him Fridays."

"What's wrong with that?" said the doctor.

"Why should Virginia be dragged along on his business trips?"

The Doctor: "Why not?"

"Oh hell, why not sleep with her too? Why not have sex with her. They're related, aren't they?"

Stanley had been shocked, but if the doctor was shocked, there was no indication; his voice just sounded steady and ordinary as he answered Mrs. Fulton, and Stanley could never understand how exactly the doctor was supposed to help a woman who said such things.

Stanley decided to leave Mannerheim a note telling him he could not do the windows. He walked across to the desk and tried to open the top drawer, for a pencil and paper. The drawer would not give; it was locked, and the lock controlled the other drawers as well. After Stanley puzzled over this, he began to wonder whether or not Mannerheim really had a one-thirty patient. Perhaps he was simply alone in his office, going over some papers. Perhaps he had shut the door to the hallway simply because he wanted privacy. In that case, Stanley would only take a minute, just long enough to tell him that he could not wash the windows. Carefully, Stanley turned the handle of the hall doorway, opening it inch by inch. He stepped tiptoe into the hallway, moving slowly. Then he became aware of Louie Stewart's voice, coming from the doctor's office.

"... so I might have to."

"Can you tell me why you think that?"

After a long pause: "I don't know."

"Was it your own idea, Louie?"

"No."

"Whose idea was it?"

"It still is an idea."

"Whose idea is it?"

A long pause.

The doctor: "Can you tell me whose idea it is if it isn't yours?"

No answer.

The doctor: "Louie, are things different than they used to be?"

No answer.

The doctor: "You usually don't lie down on the couch as you're doing now, do you?"

"No."

"Then things are a little different, aren't they?"

No answer.

"Louie, do you feel yourself under strain or tension?"

"Yes."

"You described something that was unusual to me when you first came in, can you remember?"

No answer.

"You said that shortly after Gloria Wealdon left the drug store something happened? Do you recall that?"

No answer.

The doctor again: "You said that you heard voices, Louie. Did you tell me that?"

"They don't talk any more."

"When they did, Louie, what did they say?"

"They stopped."

"You told me they stopped, but can you tell me what the voices said?"

"I'm not supposed to tell anyone."

"Did they tell you not to tell anyone?"

No answer.

"Have you ever heard them before?"

"No."

"But when Gloria Wealdon left the drug store, you heard them."

"I heard them before that."

"How soon before that, Louie?"

"Before she left. When I was filling her prescription."

"Are these voices angry with Gloria Wealdon?"

No answer.

The doctor: "Louie, is something chasing you, or after you?"

"I think so."

"Can you describe your feeling to me?"

A long pause. Then: "No, that is impossible."

"But something, someone, is after you?"

"Yes."

"Is Gloria Wealdon after you?"

"Maybe. I don't know."

"Did your voices say she was?"

"No."

"Did they tell you to do something?"

No answer.

"You're very worried about something, aren't you, Louie?"

"Yes." A long sigh.

"Can you tell me about it?"

"I don't know what to say."

"Do you find it difficult to think now?"

"Yes."

"About what?"

"My mother."

"Is something wrong with her? Is she ill?"

"She's worried about me."

"Why should she worry about you?"

"I don't know." *Pause.* "She knows me."

"Louie, would you like a few minutes' rest now?"

"I don't know."

"Do you want to rest on the couch a moment?"

"All right."

"When I come back, in a moment, we can talk some more, if you want."

No answer.

"You rest, Louie. Close your eyes and rest."

Stanley Secora moved away from the doctor's office door and hurriedly shut the door to the hallway behind him. Suddenly he felt enormous guilt at having listened to all that, and on an impulse he squeezed himself into the small utility closet in the waiting room. He could feel his back poked by a dust pan, and could hardly control his heavy breathing, his trembling. He stood in the dark, while the doctor came through the hallway door, shut it behind him, and crossed to the desk. He dialed a number and waited, while Stanley watched his back through the crack of light. After a few seconds, the doctor put the phone's arm back in its cradle. He reached for the telephone book, flipped through it, and ran his finger down a column. Then he dialed a second time. The seconds, for Stanley, were like eternities.

He heard the doctor say: "This is Jay Mannerheim. Is Dr. Baird in?"

Stanley could smell the dust around him. Now he was shaking.

"Well, let me talk to someone in authority. This is an emergency!"

Then, after another eternity: "Hello, this is Jay Mannerheim. Yes. Look, I have a patient who is very ill. It's happened quite suddenly. I think he's a catatonic schizophrenic."

The dust pan was edging off Stanley's back, off its hook. Stanley reached behind him and held it.

Mannerheim was trying not to raise his voice, but his anger was evident. "I'm not a medical doctor! I am a psychologist…. What do you mean how do I know it's a catatonic schizophrenic then! I'm telling you that's what I *think!* I need help here! … No, I have a patient at two-thirty."

Stanley was holding the dust pan now, with his back wrenched in an awkward position.

"I *can't* locate his family now," he said. "I've tried, and there's no answer…. You'll have to send a doctor here."

The dust in the utility closet seemed to increase.

Stanley heard Jay Mannerheim say his address into the telephone. He heard him say, "Believe me, this is an emergency. I can't leave this man alone."

Then Stanley sneezed, the dust pan clattered to the closet floor, and in a few, slow seconds Stanley was face-to-face with the doctor.

"What are you doing here, Stanley?"

"I burned my hands," said Stanley dumbly.

"In there?" the doctor pointed at the closet angrily.

"No. I — wanted to tell you I couldn't do the windows

today."

"What were you hiding for?"

"I — I got nervous. I — overheard s-s-s-some of — "

"Never mind now. Look, Stanley, you can do me a favor. Find Mrs. Stewart, can you do that?"

"I'm s-s-sorry, D-D-Doctor, I didn't m-mean to — "

"I know you didn't mean to. But find Mrs. Stewart, Stanley. She must be out — downtown somewhere. Find her and tell her to call me."

"Yes," said Stanley. "I'll try."

With his foot, Jay Mannerheim kicked the dust pan back inside the utility closet and shut the door quickly. "Find her, Stanley," he said before he went back into his office. "This is serious."

Twelve

"Sometimes," Fernanda said, "I wish my husband would look at another woman. But who the hell is there in this damn town?"
— FROM *Population 12,560*

Freddy Fulton had a den. Fern Fulton rarely bothered to snoop around in it, but something that had happened shortly after lunch that day made her go to the den. It was a conversation between Virginia and Freddy, one that Fern was not supposed to hear. They were still at the table in the dinette, lingering over their peachcake dessert, while Fern was clearing the table. Fern had gathered the garbage into a bag and was ready to take it out to the back yard. She had even opened the screen door, when she noticed she had forgotten to add the old bunch of philodendron to the garbage. She let the screen door swing shut and was about to reach for the philodendron when she heard her daughter say:

"I'm really worried."

"Now stop that. Your mother ..."

"She's taken the garbage out."

"Virginia, let me take care of it. Haven't I always handled things well?"

"Yes."

"Then why are you worried?"

"This is such a terrible thing to happen."

"Just because Gloria Wealdon's ..."

"I kept thinking that it wouldn't happen. That she wouldn't really come back to Cayuta."

"I know, but ..."

"Well, now it's happened."

"No one has to know, Virginia. No one."

"She'll find out. She will!"

"I've never heard you carry on like this."

"I suppose not."

"Forget it. Trust me, Virginia."

"I think we ought to warn Gloria Wealdon."

"Warn her? So she'd know for sure? You know better."

"Well, tell her, maybe, just tell her."

"Virginia, *tell* her? *Tell* her! You know better!"

"Ask her, threaten her — something."

"Oh, we'd be cooked then, all right."

"I'm afraid. If mother ever — "

"Your mother is not as hysterical about everything as you and I sometimes imagine, Virginia."

"About this?"

"Look, it's over. You and I know it's over."

"What's done is done ... but is it?"

"Let me handle it. It's my business, honey. I can handle it."

"But I've always felt involved too."

"I'll handle it. Believe me. No one has to know, no one!"

Then Fern had heard her husband push his chair back from the table and she had hurriedly given the screen door a bang. The garbage was still at her feet when her husband walked into the kitchen.

He said, "I thought you just took the garbage out."

"I had to check those clothes on the line. They're still damp."

"I'm going to the office for a while this afternoon. Not long."

"On Saturday?"

"An emergency."

"I see."

"What does that mean?"

"It means I see."

"Your voice sounded peculiar."

"Freddy, is it a serious emergency?"

"Serious enough for me to worry about, but not serious enough for you to worry about."

"Business?"

"Of course business! What would I be going to the office for if it wasn't business?"

"I don't know."

"Here, do you want some help with that garbage?"

While she was doing the dishes, Fern Fulton made a decision. She would sit Virginia down and have a long heart-to-heart talk with her. Whatever could all of it have meant? She tried to go over the whole conversation in her mind, but it was hard to remember everything in context, and even more difficult to make any sense of it. What did Gloria Wealdon have to do with any of it in the first place? She tried to think back on everything that had happened prior to lunch, after Gloria had cut back through the fields on her way home. Freddy had been puttering around in the yard until the call came from the packagers in Elbridge. He had taken the call in the kitchen. Routine conversation: yes, no, how many, when — that sort of thing; and then he had asked where Virginia was. He had gone out to the garage where she was putting away their gardening tools, and Fern had called out to both of them to clean up for lunch. There was nothing unusual about any of it. It could have happened even earlier, she decided — whatever it was that had happened; and because she had absolutely no idea what to fasten her thoughts on, she abruptly stopped what she was doing, left the un-washed dishes, and called Virginia.

There was no answer.

Freddy's Buick was gone, and then it occurred to her that he might have taken Virginia with him.

Again, she tried to think about what she had heard them say together. What?

"Gloria Wealdon ought to be warned."

"Oh, we'd be cooked then all right."

What sense did that make?

And: *"This is such a terrible thing to happen."*

She smoked a cigarette, standing up in the living room, completely in the dark about whatever it was that was taking place. Why she went to the den, she did not con-sciously know. It was an impulse. Freddy hated anyone disturbing the things in there, and it was not so much that she respected this idea, but simply that she disliked the disorder of the den. Books stacked on the floor; fishing reels falling over. Confusion. The maid had complained about it, too.

But Fern Fulton did go into the den. And she did find something there that made her heart race. She sat there smoking one cigarette after the other, reading it over and over — first with her own eyes, then with other people's eyes — until it was a senseless message, and yet one that already had some meaning for her. She didn't finish the dishes and she didn't call Freddy at the office. She just waited, and at two o'clock he came home.

When he came upstairs, he found her sitting in his yellow leather chair, in his den.

"What the — "

"Surprised?"

"I thought you were out or something."

"Freddy, did Virginia go along with you?"

"No. Why?"

"It's a wonder."

"What does that mean?"

"I mean that it's a wonder that you didn't take her along to help you solve your business emergency."

"What's the matter? Something is."

"I know it. Something is very much the matter."

"Do you want to get it off your chest?"

"I don't think it's on *my* chest."

He leaned against his desk. His face was very serious. He said, "Say it out, whatever it is, Fern."

"I've warned you before about involving Virginia in your business."

"I don't involve her in my business."

"You talk every little thing over with her, Freddy, every little thing."

"Do I?"

"You know you do. You drag her with you on your business calls, and you drag her with you out in the yard to do a man's work, and you — "

"What are you accusing me of?"

"Of giving that kid burdens she shouldn't have. She's just a kid, Freddy! A child."

"I know."

"You sound sorry. Has it all caught up with you?"

"I don't know. Maybe it has."

"Well that's news."

"She's very mature for her age, but I *have* overestimated her maturity, I suppose."

"That *is* news!"

"All right, I agree with you. What do you want to say now?"

"I want to ask you something."

"Go ahead."

"Will you be honest, Freddy?"

"Yes. I think I'll have to be."

"You won't lie?"

"No, Fern." Now his face was ashen. Fern Fulton felt her stomach do a flip. Then it was true. God, she hadn't really counted on its being true.

There was a tremor to her voice.

"Freddy, are we broke?"

"Are we *what?*"

"Are we ruined? Wiped out?"

He looked at her for a moment, and then he began to laugh. He threw his head back and began to laugh and laugh. Fern sat there, waiting. Finally, when he could speak, he said, "Where did you *ever* get that idea?"

"Is it true?"

"No, no, it is not true. Whatever made you think it was?"

"You swear that to me. You're not trying to hide that from me, to spare me?"

"We are solvent, Fern. We are better than solvent. We're damn near rich." He was laughing again.

"Because if you ever went to Gloria Wealdon and asked her for money, Freddy, I wouldn't be able to hold up my head in Cayuta."

"Nor would I," he giggled.

"I know she's rich, and we're good friends, but Freddy, she hurt me with that book. She honest-to-God hurt me."

He said more seriously, "I know that, Fern."

"Do you?"

"Yes, I do. And I'm sorry about that."

"I believe you actually are."

"About that, and about a lot of things, Fern."

"You're being sincere, aren't you?'

"Yes. And I'm sorry, too, that you have to ask if I am. I'm going to make things a little different around here. I hadn't planned to say it. I don't like to say things. It spoils it."

"Not for me."

"I know not for you…. A long time ago, Min Stewart said you had spirit — said you had a way of speaking out that she admired."

"Min said that?"

"Yes."

"When?"

"I don't remember. Once."

"You never told me Min said that."

"Well, she did."

"Why didn't you ever tell me, Freddy? I always knew Min was a loyal friend. Now there's a friend for you!"

"Well, anyway — "

"Min said I had spirit, huh?" Fern Fulton beamed.

"What made you think we were broke, Fern?"

"Huh?"

"What you were saying earlier."

"Oh! This!" She fished in the pocket of her apron and brought out the wrinkled piece of paper she'd been folding and unfolding since one o'clock. "What does this mean."

She read the note aloud.

> "*I am worried about Elbridge, and its effect on mother. Gloria Wealdon is the only answer. I can do it better than you can, even if threats are vulgar where there is no way to carry them out. I'll find a way. Don't worry. V.*"

"Where was it?" said Freddy.

"On your desk — right there on your desk. You can see why — "

"When did you get it? Find it. When did you find it?"

"Just a while ago, not long ago. Why? What's the matter?"

"I don't have time to explain."

"Where are you going?"

"I'm going to find Gloria Wealdon," Freddy said. "I'm going to find Virginia," he said. He was already running down the stairs when he added the words, "To stop her."

Thirteen

Gina knew she was no intellectual. Even in college she had been a poor student, but she had heart. What else mattered? And she had discovered very early in life that a simple "Yes" in response to someone's question, "Have you read much Dostoyevsky?" could go a long way. A bluff was better than a brain; half of living was bluffing anyway.
— FROM *Population 12,360*

Midway through her veal knuckle, Gloria Wealdon had felt far too ill to continue the luncheon with Min Stewart. She had excused herself and driven home. As she was coming out of the garage, she was startled by the sudden appearance of Freddy Fulton.

"Milo's at school," she said, "at the track meet." In addition to the severe stomach ache, she felt a coldness toward Fern's husband upon recalling her conversation with Fern that noon.

"I wasn't looking for Milo."

"I'm not feeling very well."

"You haven't seen Virginia?"

"Not since this noon at your place."

"We're anxious to find her, to tell her something. If she comes around, by any chance, would you tell her we're anxious to reach her?"

"I don't think she'll come around," said Gloria. "She never has."

"But you will remember if she does?"

"Sounds like life and death."

Freddy made a noise that was meant to sound like laughter, but which sounded grotesque and inhuman. He followed Gloria to the front screen door. "You were supposed to have lunch with Min today, weren't you?"

"I just came from the hotel," Gloria said. "I feel lousy."

"Oh, the hotel!"

"Yes," said Gloria.

"Do you know what Min — "

But Freddy was already on his way across the lawn, running.

She was just as glad. She was in no mood to have a conversation with anyone, much less him.

Once she was inside, she kicked off her heels and slipped her feet into the space shoes. Then she plopped on the chair beside the telephone and picked up her clipboard. She had remembered to buy the stamps and the tissue paper, but she would have to order the olives and the wine.

As she dialed, she studied her notes again:

NOTES FOR A NOVEL ABOUT A WOMAN
WHOSE BOOK HITS THE BEST SELLER LIST

She looked at number three a second time.

3. Minnie Stewart asking me for lunch despite fact I had plenty in book about Louie. What want? Apologize to me for past behave?

The grocer asked her to wait when he answered, and she took the pencil attached to the board and wrote:

*M. S. says L. off his rocker. Don't believe. Expects
me to crawl to him, but has audacity to refuse me
b-club. Bunk about my life in danger! Wants own
way. Won't give inch! g.d. snob!"*

As she gave the grocer her order, a headache began its
slow warm-up, a small, painful pulsating somewhere near
the thalamus.

She continued to write while she spoke to the grocer.

*What is it about people with money? I have now,
but still I not like them ... Intrinsic something ...
P. that way too ... How about book called RICH
ARE DIFFERENT? ... THE RICH ARE DIF-
FERENT by Gloria Wealdon.*

THE RICH ARE DIFFERENT
by Gloria Wealdon

Gloria Wealdon's
THE RICH ARE DIFFERENT

While the grocer went to check on whether or not there
was fresh asparagus, Gloria Wealdon shut her eyes and
tried to remember that thing F. Scott Fitzgerald had written
about the rich; how had it gone?

*Let me tell you about the very rich. They are different
from you and me.... Even when they enter into our world,
or sink below us....*

But that was all she could remember.

*Even when they enter into our world, or sink below
us....*

She tried to remember Min Stewart sinking below her;
tried to remember just one social incident in which Min
had sunk, but instead she saw only her own hand-flailing,
remembered only her own descents.... Like the one that

very noon, at lunch.

She had been complaining to Min about her dinner party that evening for Pitts, by way of letting Min know that her literary agent was arriving from New York. She did not bother to tell her that there were to be only three at the most for dinner (though Milo claimed he was not going to attend, Gloria had no such high hopes for the evening); instead, she pretended to be worried about what to serve. She liked herself immensely for thinking to bring up the subject. In light of Min's prior conversation, it was deliciously anti-climactic and its saccharine defiance delighted her, though Min Stewart never seemed to show the effect of any new tack — her face was always composed and enigmatic.

Min said, "I have with me a very good cookbook, *The Williamsburg Art of Cookery.* Do you know it?"

"I don't know. Let me see it?"

"*Now,* Mrs. Wealdon? You haven't even — "

"I eat very little for lunch ever," said Gloria. She popped the anti-acid pill Milo had given her into her mouth and swallowed it with water. She reached for the book Min handed her.

Min said, "The binding is worn. I'm taking it to Stanley's for mending. It was printed in the year 1742."

Gloria accepted it from her and began leafing through it.

Min continued: "I shouldn't call it *The Williamsburg Art of Cookery,* because actually that book is a pretense at being this one."

Gloria read the title: *The Accomplifh'd Gentlewoman's Companion.* In the book's ancient typography, the ligature *s* looked like an *f.* Gloria said, "It sounds like the author lisped."

Min ignored the remark. She said, "They're very old recipes, and they sound quite complicated, but it shouldn't deceive you. They're all of them very sound."

"They even broiled steaks in those days," said Gloria. It seemed odd, somehow, for people to broil steaks back in the 1700's.

"They're particularly sound on steaks. They suggest that a few hot coals from the fire be placed into a chafing dish, and that when the steaks are done they be placed into the hot dish and served hot to table. They advise you not to turn the steak either, until one side is done. Today most people turn them back and forth."

"Oh, Lord!"

"What?"

"Here," Gloria said, "under 'Confectionery.' Well, really! And everyone talks about how wicked we're supposed to be *now.*"

"What are you talking about, Mrs. Wealdon?"

"Just read this poem," said Gloria. "Just read these first three lines. *I'd* never get away with this kind of thing, but I suppose it's all right, if it's in a cookbook. Honestly!"

"I have no idea what you're talking about. Give it to me, please."

"I'm *going* to," Gloria said with some irritation. "It was *you* who were talking earlier about patience being the pace of nature or something."

"It isn't impatience so much," said Min Stewart, "as it is the fact that we have nothing in common as a basis for further discussion, until you tell me what this discussion concerns."

"These lines," Gloria said. "Read them. The ones about the veal and the cows."

She watched Min Stewart as she read. "How do you like that? If I wrote that word in a book, they'd take a good sharp black pencil to it, but I suppose because it's in a cookbook it's all right. Well, I don't think it's all right. I think it's ludicrous, and it's a ludicrous idea! Who cares what the veal was doing before it was to be eaten, or to how many cows? Preposterous! I couldn't get any ideas from that book, Mrs. Stewart. I'd get sick to my stomach."

Min Stewart smiled. "But you are already, aren't you?"

"I have a nervous stomach, yes."

"I'm sorry," said Min Stewart. Then she said, "I'm familiar with the portion you object to. It was a verse written by St. George Tucker to his friend, a Mr. Lomax, when the latter failed to avail himself of an invitation to visit him for dinner."

"That excuses it?"

"It needs no excuse, Mrs. Wealdon. The word is *sucked.* Had you read along in the verse, just to the next line, you would have understood. The next line is this: 'Lamb that was fattened in a' — and I'll spell it — 'h-o-u-f-e.'"

"I don't know what that proves," said Gloria. "A misprint?"

"No. It proves, Mrs. Wealdon, that in that day the letter *s,* when printed in combination with certain other letters, appeared as *f.* At any rate, to our eyes it looks like an *f.* It's the old style, that's all. The word was not the word you think. The veal, you see, was to have fed on cow's milk before being slaughtered."

Min smiled.

Gloria handed back the cookbook. Her face felt hot with shame and embarrassment. How many many many times in the past had this sort of thing happened to her! If she had only thought, if she had only waited a moment before she spoke, she would have seen her error, but she had let impulse carry her headlong into disaster. "How would I have known that, anyway?" she murmured, knowing full well she should have known that; knowing too that she would have, if only she had not been so bent on challenging Min, challenging her in any way, even challenging her cookbook.

"You wouldn't have known, of course," said Min Stewart, "not without having learned it somewhere, or having

been warned of it ... The last lines of that verse are particularly pleasant to think of in terms of a sumptuous
dinner party."

She quoted the lines:

> *Madeira filled each Chink and Cleft*
> *We ate, we drank, we went to bed,*
> *And flept as though we all were dead.*

She pronounced the letter as an *f*, in *flept*.

Then she placed the book beside her coat, and continued
eating her shad roe.

"I should have warned you about *that* too," she said,
"but my mind was largely on my earlier warning. It still
is, Mrs. Wealdon. I wouldn't want *you* to *fleep* as though
you were dead, not when the likelihood of your actually
being dead looms so large. Louie is all I have, and I want
to keep him with me."

After Gloria Wealdon finished giving her grocery order,
she lifted the receiver again to order the wine. She lit a
cigarette, and tried desperately to recall the name of the
wine Pitts liked. With her pencil, doodling on the clipboard, she wrote:

> *you don't fcare me Min, fo there!*

"Would Tavel be the name of the rosé, Mrs. Wealdon?"
the liquor dealer's voice asked.

"I think it is, by gum!" she said.

"Yes, m'am. All right, m'am."

Hanging up, sucking the smoke into her lungs, Gloria
held her head where the pain seemed pinpointed.

She hoped Milo carried out his threat not to appear at
dinner.

She could hear him now, droning on in that dull way of

his. She shut her eyes and his voice came to her mind as
fresh and alive as it was at all the countless dinner parties
and luncheons and cocktail hours when he would be saying:

"Oh yes, often the botanical name is pretty, but the
common names for rock plants have a certain flair, like
amur adonis, prickly-thrift, whitlow grass, navelseed, toadflax, houseleek or moonwort. They're weird, strange, delightful sounds, aren't they, like — "

And in her head now, she could not stop his voice calling
out the common names of rock plants.

Gloria fumbled in her bucket bag for the new bottle of
anti-acid pills. She got a glass of water from the kitchen,
and a bottle of aspirin. As she settled down in the huge
Morris chair by the window, she saw Secora's manuscript
and the piece of coconut ice. The latter she took after
swallowing her pills, as a reward for swallowing them,
and she thought of the way Milo always felt guilty about
eating sweets; she thought of him that morning when she
had seen him pocket one of the candies Stanley had
brought, how flushed his face had become when he realized she was watching him. She imagined him off in some
corner of the school gymnasium, eating his sweet in secret,
like a tom-cat behind an ashcan in an alley with a fish
head.

When P. got there she would tell him that about Milo
and sweets; when P. got there she would tell him everything; and wouldn't everything be all right then.

The thought gave her some solace, but she was tired
now, and aching. She needed to curl up under the blanket
on her bed. She would like to spend these hours between
now and Pitts' arrival as though unborn, huddling in the
warm, dark protectiveness of her beige comforter. She remembered how last fall Milo had taken those bouvardia
roots and planted them in the flats of sand and peat moss
in the basement; she remembered the way suddenly one

day near Christmas she had seen the huge, waxy, orange-blossom-scented flowers in the living room, and she'd said, "Where did these come from?" and Milo'd said, "They're the bouvardia in bloom at last."

She would be like the bouvardia when Pitts arrived. She got up from the Morris chair and wandered wearily into the bedroom. She left Secora's manuscript on the endtable; she hurt too badly now to read in bed, or to do anything but curl there until her pills took effect. Kicking off her space shoes and pulling her girdle down, she opened the closet door to toss them in. She should have laughed at what she saw then; she should not have been afraid at all in light of all that had happened at lunch; but sometimes a sudden crazy unlikelihood, such as finding Virginia Fulton pressed against your dresses in your closet on a sunny May afternoon for no reason, was even more terrifying than the thought of Louie Stewart hunting you to murder you by dark.

Fourteen

People in the town had facial expressions that
were almost wax-fixed, showing no emotion, like
the faces of the dead, for everything that happened
to them was like life under a rock — with the rock
never letting on about the crawling world it hid.
   — FROM *Population 12,360*

He found her in the lobby of the hotel.

She said, "Why, Frederick, what are you doing here?"

"Looking for you," he said.

"How flattering!" Min Stewart beamed.

Freddy Fulton took her arm, guiding her toward the rear door, which led to the parking lot. "My car's outside."

"Service with a smile," said Min. "Except that you don't

seem to be smiling very much this afternoon, Frederick."

"Min, have you seen Virginia?"

"No."

"I'm in quite a state."

"I can see that you are."

"May I drop you somewhere?"

"As a matter of fact," said Min Stewart, "I've been thinking of calling for Louie at Jay Mannerheim's office." She looked at her watch. "It's two-fifteen now. He should be free in another fifteen minutes. But I don't mind waiting." She chuckled. "In fact, I rather enjoy thumbing through all of Jay's magazines."

"My car's over there," Freddy Fulton said.

"I had a lovely shad for lunch. Have you eaten at the hotel recently, Frederick? The food's quite good. It's a change from Oswald Ripley's management!"

"I haven't, but Fern has. She gave me the same report."

"Oh, it's quite agreeable now."

"It's about time," said Fulton.

"Yes. Yes," Min Stewart nodded.

When he slammed the door shut, after getting Min in on the other side, he faced her, and she nodded again. But this time it was different. It was a gesture that said, "I understand."

"Trouble," was all Freddy said. He started the car. "Shall we go right to Jay's?"

"Yes, we'd better, unless you have — "

"Min, I don't know what I have. I just wish Gloria Wealdon had stayed away!"

"Have you seen her since she had lunch with me?"

"Yes."

Min said, "I see."

"I'm worried about Virginia. I thought Virginia might have tried to get hold of Gloria. Now I don't know what to think. I'm afraid to think."

"I don't understand," said Min.

"I know you don't, Min."

"What has Virginia got to do with it?"

"I'm going to have to tell you something that I don't want to tell you, but you're the only person I can tell."

"It sounds serious, Frederick."

"It is, Min. I think I'll just tell you — just tell you everything, without any explanations or embellishments. Is that all right?"

"Do you mean without any *excuses* or embellishments?"

"I suppose I do mean that," said Freddy Fulton, "I might as well say what I mean from the beginning."

Min Stewart sat back in the Packard's front seat, stared straight ahead, and placed her hands in her lap. "Continue," she said.

At the Cayuta Retreat, one of the switchboard operators guffawed at the male nurse's joke. "'At's good," he said, "so long as you love your mother, huh? Boy, that's funny! So long as you love your mother! What you got to worry about, huh? So long as you love your mother! Oh boy!"

"Take your call," said the nurse.

"As if I don't know who it's going to be," the switchboard operator said. He yanked the plug out and then in. "Cayuta Retreat," he said.

He made a face of exaggerated patience. "Yes, Dr. Mannerheim." He said, "I am not the man in charge here. I only work the board, Dr. Mannerheim, so don't sound off at me, see! ... Yeah, yeah, I know that, and so does Dr. Waterman know it, and we're going to take care of you just as soon as — "

He held the arm of the phone out while the voice continued to rage. He yawned for the benefit of the male nurse, then pretended to plug his ears.

Then the switchboard operator said, "As soon as possible, Dr. Mannerheim. Yes, sir. Yes, sir. Right away, sir. Of course, sir. Anything you say, sir. Goodbye, sir," hanging up the phone. "And go to hell, sir!" he shouted at the instrument.

He said to the male nurse, "Can you imagine that? Calls up and tells us he's got a catalonic schizophrenic over there we should come and get! Nerve!"

"Catatonic."

"Huh? Okay, catatonic, catalonic, cataschmonic ... so long as he loves his mother, huh?" he laughed at that for quite a few seconds.

"Mannerheim, huh?"

"Yeah. He's not even a doctor."

"He's a psychologist. They don't have to be doctors."

"They don't have to call up and chew me out neither. What can *I* do? Do I own the Retreat?"

"Did Dr. Waterman do anything about it?"

"He will."

"How many times has he called?"

"Three, four — how do I know? He thinks he's some kinda big deal. I got a catalonic schizophrenic over here, he says. So *I* gotta common cold!"

"I heard he lost some patients because of that book."

"Yeah?" The switchboard operator made an obscene gesture. "He shouldn't fool around then."

"Not because of that. Because of the part about income tax."

"Yeah? I don't remember," he said. "That's a part I musta skipped."

"Naturally," the male nurse laughed. He said, "People around here were taking him off their income tax. You know. Medical expense."

"So?"

"Well, it's the way you said. He's not a doctor. It's against the law."

"No kidding?"

"He's not doing anything wrong, see? It's just that the law says an M.D. has to head-shrink you, if you want it off your tax."

"I don't go for that psychoalley stuff."

"A while back I had an idea to massage people," said the male nurse, "relax them and everything. Go right to their homes."

"Yeah?"

"Heck, I'm a nurse, aren't I? So why couldn't people take it off their income tax? I'd be giving them help, wouldn't I?"

"I don't know," said the switchboard operator. "I wouldn't let you near *my* wife."

"This would be for men, too, don't you get it? I mean, I'd massage men, too!"

"Come to think of it," said the switchboard operator, "I wouldn't let you near me either."

"Oh, *you'd* have a lot to worry about, *you* would."

"Th-ure, why not? Th-ome people think I'm adorable!"

The pair laughed at the switchboard operator's swishy inflection.

"Anyway," said the nurse after, "it wouldn't have been deductible. I asked around and Bill Farley down at City Hall told me no dice."

From around the corner, a man in a dark blue suit appeared.

"What about that ambulance for Mannerheim?" he asked the switchboard operator.

"None's gone yet, Dr. Waterman."

"Do you want to go along on this one?" the doctor asked the nurse.

"Sure."

"Call Number Three and tell them to go there," the doctor said, "and check that address. I think it might be his home address. It's Saturday."

"It's his office address," said the switchboard operator. "Check on it anyway."

The doctor left through the revolving door.

"Just your luck," the switchboard operator said. "You get to wrestle with some nut on a hot afternoon in May."

"Catatonics are usually quiet."

"Yeah?"

"Real vegetables. The ones that sit around on the wards in the same position."

"Ready to pick up: one vegetable," said the switchboard operator as he dialed.

"Besides, I'd rather be out on a call then sitting around here."

"Was' the matter, lover, don't you thee I think you're thwell?" the switchboard operator laughed.

Then he said, "Hello, Dr. Mannerheim? This is the Cayuta Re — What?"

He listened a moment, and then he put down the phone in its cradle. "Well!" he said.

"What's the matter?"

"He flew the coop," said the switchboard operator. "The catalonic took off on the doctor."

"Great! I'll bet Mannerheim's steamed."

"Real steamed, buddy-boy," said the switchboard operator. "Very very steamed! Well, so," he fished under the counter for *Life* Magazine, "should it work my blood pressure up because there's another nut loose? So long as I love my mother, isn't that right, nurse?"

Fifteen

… but Gina knew one thing — she was going to win her battle with this town — even if she had to fight dirty! In the end, she was going to win!
— FROM *Population 12,360*

Stanley Secora could not find Min Stewart for the doctor. He looked for her in the drug store, but she was not there;

no one knew where she was. Twice he telephoned her from the drug store. After each call, he retrieved the dime in the coin-return slot and used it to try Gloria Wealdon's number.

When eventually he decided to go directly to the Wealdons', he had in mind no thought of protecting her from Louie Stewart. Despite all he had heard in the doctor's office, he felt that Louie was in good hands, that soon the funny-farm would come and get him and lock him up.

His decision to go to the Wealdons' was the same impulsive sort of bravado which had stayed him in all the strange-sounding towns of the war, back when he was a hero, young, and such a crazy fighter ("You dumb Polack," they used to say, laughing with him, clapping their hands across his back. "You dumb, death-happy Polack!") in Santa Maria Infante, San Pietro, Monte Cerri, Monte Branchi, Gaeta, Cisterna — in all of them.

To Stanley Secora the truth of loving was touching. What you could not touch, you could not love; and when you fell in love, you wanted to touch and you wanted to perform intercourse (Stanley always phrased it that way, because all he knew about the "act" — another of his phrases — he had read in volumes on sexology). That was love. That was what he wanted when he got to Gloria Wealdon's, and that was why he was going there now: to get what he wanted.

Yet he did not appear to be stalking a victim; he was not striding toward his destination with his shoulders squared and his jaw set; he was nearly rubber-kneed with the weakness that flooded through him, and he was trembling. Over and over, as he went down Alden Avenue toward the blue house at the end of the street, he had to stop and wipe off his glasses, because they were steaming, and he was afraid.

In the war, he *had* been brave. He had done crazy, wild,

unbelievably courageous things, but then as now he had been terrified. Once he had been ordered to stay in an area where a number of men had been killed by a mortar shell (he could remember that, after the order had been given, a buddy had said, "You're expendable, Secora. In other words you're expendable" — but Stanley had not known what the word meant). He had sat out the watches alone in the dark and in the day, and he had not been afraid until there was the smell. That smell. He had heard that bodies left dead had a horrible odor, and that was it; and once or twice he had looked at them lying around him there, and he had found out something else about dead bodies that no one had ever told him, that he had never heard anywhere. Some of them bloated. He saw one bloated in the sun one morning just after he woke up. It had bust its buttons and had turned blue, and its skin was peeling. Its name was Private Carlton Phillips, and it had gone to Harvard, and that's what everyone had called him, "Harvard," and after Stanley had seen him, he had run away from where he had been ordered to stay. But for a long time after that day, that year, he could still remember the smell and the sight of the buttons popping in the sun on the corpse's uniform.

So he knew fear. That was why his courage had to be so wild and crazy, because he knew the size of his fear, and that it was awfully big.

Today, going after love, Stanley could not visualize or even think of how love would be accomplished. Whenever he tried to do that, he either thought of those line illustrations from chapter six on positions for intercourse in his sexology book, or he thought of the character Will from *Population 12,360* — Will with the perspiration running down his well-tanned back and the grass in the cuffs of his white pants, and Gina, the heroine, saying, "Rip off my clothes and make me naked." Stanley knew that if anyone ever said that to him, he would faint with embarrassment.

Today, going after Love, Stanley was unsure of himself, more so than ever because of that morning; but it was this very feeling of being unsure that made him determined to do it. He had to.

When he arrived at the Wealdons', the first thing he noticed was that her car was in the garage. She was home.

He wiped off his glasses a fourth time since being on the street, and then walked to the front door and pushed the bell.

He said, "Mrs. Wealdon?"

No answer.

He pushed the doorbell again.

"Mrs. Wealdon, please? Are you home?"

He stood there shuffling his feet, listening to the silence, and though he rang again and again, he was convinced she was not inside. He glanced at his watch. It was two-forty. He knew that Milo's track meet would be on now and that he would be there at the high school. Mrs. Wealdon was probably just somewhere in the neighborhood.

When he tried the front screen door, it was locked.

Stanley went around to the back door, the one off the garage. He opened it very carefully, and shut it gently behind him without making any noise. He tiptoed across to a kitchen chair and sat down. He took off both his shoes and placed them neatly under the chair. He loosened his tie, and as he did this the idea came to him to take his shirt off. Like Will, in the book.

He had no course of action planned exactly. He unbuttoned his shirt and hung it over the back of the chair. He pulled his belt in another notch, and then wished he could take off his glasses, but he was quite blind without them.

He decided the best idea would be to wait for her in the living room, in the semi-darkness. He could sit in one of the armchairs, and when she came in he could just get up and say, "Hi, there." In his hand he could have a piece of the candy he had made her, and he could say, "Like a sweet?"

When he heard the car stop in front of the house, he ducked behind a curtain and looked out.

It was Freddy Fulton and Min Stewart was with him.

He decided not to move, but simply to stay there while they rang the doorbell and discovered she was not home. And then another car arrived. Stanley saw Jay Mannerheim behind the wheel.

Instantly, he was afraid. Mannerheim always frightened him a little. He wondered why the doctor was here. To find Min Stewart, of course — but what then? And he thought of the way Jay Mannerheim always used the telephone. He thought of the unlocked door in the kitchen, of his shoes there, and his shirt.

As quickly as he could, Stanley ran back and pushed the trigger-lock shut. He took his shirt and his shoes and as he darted back toward the living room with them, his socks slid on the slippery linoleum and he fell. His glasses flew from his ears and were swept across the floor.... Where?

He tried to feel for them with his hands, but it was no good. A part of the bandage on his hand came unraveled, and he tried to tuck the stray piece back inside. It would not stay. He was on all fours when he heard the sharp ding-dong — the front bell.

Min Stewart said, "He doesn't drive. It's fortunate that he does not know how to drive or he might have taken one of the cars and beat us here."

"He could have just as easily gotten a ride," said Freddy Fulton.

"I don't think either of you understand Louie's condition," said Jay Mannerheim. "I'm not too worried about him where Gloria Wealdon's concerned."

"What does not *too* worried about him mean, Jay?" said Min.

The doorbell rang sharply.

Stanley lay flat now. He could not tell how much of him could be seen if someone were to look in the front screen door. He thought he remembered that it was not possible to see beyond the entrance way from the front porch, but without his glasses he could only rely on his memory — and had he remembered right?

"It means that I think we're being alarmists," said Jay. "He wouldn't go after Gloria. It's too obvious."

Stanley began to slide on his belly toward the living room, dragging his shoes and shirt. He had to get out of sight; that was the first thing. He had to be somewhere else if Mannerheim were to come around to the back door and look in. At least he had been able to lock it; that was luck.

"What if I just run down and check and see if Virginia's home?" Freddy Fulton said.

"Mrs. Wealdon obviously isn't in," said Mannerheim. "I think we'd better get on the ball and start looking for Louie."

Someone pushed the doorbell again. "Her car is in, Jay."

"I know, Min, but she could be anyplace."

"And so could Louie, Jay."

"Well, he's not here."

"How do we know? And how do we know he's not on his way here?"

"We don't, of course, Min."

Another ring of the doorbell.

"But I doubt it."

"I ought to call Fern and see if Virginia's back," said Freddy.

"Couldn't we use *her* phone, Jay?" Min Stewart.

"You mean just walk in?"

The sound of the screen door being tried.

"It is an emergency, Jay."

"Yes, and I could call Fern from here instead of having

to go there. If Virginia isn't there, I'm going to Elbridge."

Min Stewart said, "I think that's wise. I think you'll find her there."

"Where?" said Mannerheim. "Who?"

"No one," Min Stewart said. "Just Virginia. Frederick's upset about her."

"Well, this door is locked. I suppose I could try the back door, but I don't feel right about it."

"Try, Jay. Louie may even have gone to the drug store. I just think we could accomplish so much if we simply had access to a telephone."

"All right, I'll go around back."

Stanley Secora came to what felt like a step leading off the living room. He felt it with his hands; it was the pair of steps leading up to the rest of the house. He remembered now. He eased himself up, pulling more of his bandage loose. He was afraid Mannerheim would force his way in now; he had to find a place to hide — a place away from the living room.

"Don't say anything to Jay about Elbridge," said Freddy Fulton at the front door.

Min said, "I am one of the few females in Cayuta who finds the idea of Jay Mannerheim's being my confessor completely repulsive."

Freddy Fulton laughed. Then he said, "Oh God, I'm worried, Min."

"We're both worried, Frederick. I can't help thinking Jay could somehow have prevented Louie's running off that way. And I'm absolutely positive that he must have provoked Louie. Louie never runs away … not unless — "

"Unless what?"

"Unless he really has been driven too far, as I suspected. Then he'll be here, you can be sure of that. He'll come to this house *after* her."

"Min, we're both worked up. We've got to just keep calm."

"Do you think Virginia would harm anyone?"

"No. I'm almost certain she wouldn't. She's not like that."

"You've put her through a great deal, Frederick, for a little girl."

"I know … but she just wouldn't do anything violent."

From the back door came another chime and then Jay Mannerheim's voice: "Gloria Wealdon? Hello? Anyone home?"

At the front door, Min Stewart said quietly, "You believe your child is incapable of violence, and I'm so sure that mine is thoroughly capable of it. It will be interesting — "

"Interesting?" Freddy Fulton said in a sick tone. "Oh, God, I just wish she was here. I wish she was where I knew she was safe."

"You mean Gloria Wealdon?"

"No, Virginia."

"But Gloria Wealdon's safety is more important at this moment, when you think about it," said Min Stewart.

Stanley was easing himself over the top step and sliding on his belly down the hall, when he heard Mannerheim shout to those at the front of the house.

"Okay, I'll try some windows. The door is locked."

Stanley felt along the walls until he came to a room. It would be the bedroom, the master bedroom; he could remember doing the windows — it was the first room on the hall. He crawled inside, bumping his head against a chair. He dropped his shirt and struggled with his shoes to get them on. He put his shirt on too, and then remembered that he had left his tie behind, probably on the kitchen table. He felt even more afraid; it did not occur to him that it was not very likely that Mannerheim would know a tie of his from a tie of Milo's. He only thought of his tie there, and Mannerheim's seeing it; or of a sudden crunching sound, as Mannerheim's foot came down on his glasses, somewhere on the kitchen floor. Anyone, almost anyone in Cayuta, New York, would know Stanley Secora's glasses on sight. They were the thickest in Kantogee County. He was positive of that. That was another souvenir from the war, the one he displayed most prominently of all.

Then he heard Jay Mannerheim's voice inside, on the lower level. He was walking toward the front door.

"She'll probably turn us in as housebreakers," said Jay. "I believe she'd do it. Look, I'm going to alert the police about Louie, Min."

"Not the police. He is not a criminal yet, Jay."

"Not to pull him in for anything, just to help us find him, Min. Look, I'm telling you, he's a very sick boy. He's cracked up. Does that *mean* anything to you? He's not the way you remember him this morning."

"Just let me call Fern," said Freddy Fulton.

"Not the police, Jay," Min Stewart said.

Stanley heard someone dial a number; and he heard Min Stewart continue to protest to Jay Mannerheim that the police were not to be called. Stanley tried to squint to see where a chair was, where he could sit and wait.

While he carefully eased himself up off the floor, he heard Freddy Fulton say, "She's not home. Fern's worried sick."

"You'd better go to Elbridge, Frederick."

"Yes, I'd better, hadn't I?"

"Yes."

In the background, Jay Mannerheim was on the telephone.

Min Stewart said, "Don't worry about me. I'll wait here for Louie. He'll come here."

"I don't like to leave you, but — "

"Hurry along, you poor man," said Min. "You're frantic, Frederick. Go along and find her, and don't feel so badly. We are none of us flawless."

"Thank you, Min."

Stanley was on his feet now, feeling his way along the bureau in the master bedroom.

"He's not at the drug store," he heard Mannerheim say, "Min, let me call the police."

"I know my boy. He'll come here."

"I know that you know your boy, Min, but please let me point out that Louie isn't your boy right now — not the boy you know. He's very ill. He's not predictable now."

"It was you who said you weren't worried about him."

"I meant I don't think he'll come here."

"Where then?"

"I honestly don't know."

"Then he *could* come here?"

"He *could*."

"I'll wait here, then."

"As you like, Min, but I have to call the police. This is my responsibility. I'm his doctor."

"Doctor?"

Min chuckled.

"Yes *doctor,* Min. I'm fully qualified for my work."

"Do you know the word defensive, Doctor? I believe it's part of the psychological jargon?"

The doctor was dialing the telephone. Stanley's hands left the bureau and he came to the long mirror on the back of the closet. He could feel the arm of a chair; he knew that just beyond that there would be the bed. He could crawl under the bed.

As he was reaching for the chair, he heard Fern Fulton's voice. "That's what I'd like to know," she was shouting. "How about it, Min?"

"Fern, there is nothing going on. We are concerned about my son."

"Where's Glo?"

"Somewhere. In the neighborhood, I suppose, though she was ill at lunch. It was probably an excuse."

Stanley passed from one arm of the chair to the other. With his foot, he felt the edge of the bed.

"Was Freddy here?"

"Shhh, the doctor is calling the police."

"The police? What's going on around here?"

"Now look," Jay Mannerheim said, "I can't talk with you two shouting behind me. Now shut up!"

Stanley smiled. That told them. He began to inch his way toward the bed, his hands flailing the air for the first of the four posts.

He heard Fern Fulton start up again: "Well, there's Glo's bag."

"Yes, the one she had at lunch."

"Then she's probably right in the neighborhood."

"That's what we think."

"I wish I knew why Freddy's so worried about Virginia. She's only been gone for a short time. She's taken her bicycle and gone for hours on end and he never — But then there was this note."

"What note?"

"Oh, it's all senseless," said Fern Fulton.

Stanley found the post and clung to it. He eased himself down on the bed.

"All right," he heard Jay Mannerheim say. "The police are alerted. We'll have him rounded up in no time."

"He's not a cow, Jay."

"Who?" said Fern Fulton. "Is Louie in trouble?"

It was at this point that Stanley Secora felt her leg. He touched the stocking, and his hand shot back as though he had put it on a hot griddle. Her leg! She was lying on the bed — all this time!

"Fern, now you go home," Jay Mannerheim was saying. "You're just confusing everything."

"She's not confusing me," said Min Stewart.

"Thank you, Min."

"Oh, for the love of God, do any of you realize we have no right inside Gloria Wealdon's house!"

"Gloria Wealdon's house," said Min Stewart. "It's Milo Wealdon's house, thank you. He built it and paid for it, and it's his house."

"She could build a palace with what she's made," said Fern Fulton. "She could build a — whatayoucallit — a villa or something, with all the money she's made!"

Stanley brought his hand up her leg, up to the knee. She was asleep. He smiled. He felt his way along the side of the bed.

"Fern," said Jay Mannerheim, "I think you really should go home."

"I suppose you call this mixing socially, hmmm Jay?"

"No, I don't! It's just that — "

"Oh, isn't he supposed to mix socially with anyone?" Min Stewart.

"Not with a patient," said Fern Fulton. "Didn't you know I was having my head shrunk, Min?"

"Really?"

"Listen," Jay Mannerheim said, "I don't ..."

And Stanley Secora was kneeling, his hands were on her throat, his fingers were traveling up toward her mouth, when suddenly he knew. He felt the wet squishiness on his bandages, and he felt the cold. He lifted one of her arms, and its weight was too heavy; and when he brought his hands back to cover the sound about to come from him, he smelled the vomit that was smeared on the bandages. He smelled it, and it was just a sour, ugly odor; but in the dark, there in the Wealdons' master bedroom, where he could not see, where he was trapped with it, caught there with it like an animal in a cage, it became not just an odor of vomit, but that other odor ... that death smell. And the sound came screaming out of his big, shock-struck body, so loud it terrified even him, so high and unlikely it was like a girl's, and the sound said such a crazy word — just "Harrrrr-verd!"; Harvard was all; just that in such a funny way, like some old she-ghost wailing in the yard at Cambridge.

Sixteen

... and the town sat in the lush hills of the Finger Lakes, sat like an unsightly red pimple on the soft, white back of some sultry and voluptuous woman.
— FROM *Population 12,360*

Pitts Ralei drove north on Route 2. In an hour he would be in Cayuta. As he drove, he kept remembering the way the book that had made him a rich man began. Like the rest of the book, the opening sentence was doubtless not destined to be remembered in the hereafter, but it did promise a quick thrill for those less concerned with immortality. And *Population 12,360* lived up to its opening sentence's promise. It delivered a bitter exposé of a thinly-disguised small town — seasoned generously with sex. It was a very bad book when viewed as literature. In manuscript the grammatical errors, the errors of spelling, and all the other unbelievable errors of fact in place and time were overwhelming, but Pitts Ralei could see beyond them. What he saw was a best seller. The kind of book that would send all the middle-aged women in this country reeling back from their homes to their rental libraries, with their faces flushed from reading it, murmuring what trash it was, pretending to be angry for ever having placed themselves on the waiting list for it; the kind of book that would be made into a movie, that the pocketbook publishers would pay upwards of $100,000 for; the kind of book agents dreamed of one day finding in the slush on their desks. Nine months after he had agreed to represent

Gloria Wealdon, the book began to fulfill Ralei's dreams.

Now, if he could only continue to keep everything under control, the future would be absolutely iridescent.

Pitts was slightly amazed — and terribly amused — by this woman. He did not love her; she was as far from the sort of love object he would choose for himself as her book was from the sort of book he would choose to read, yet the fact remained he had broken his rule about never becoming involved with clients. Shortly after they had met, one night when he had asked her for a before-dinner drink at his apartment, she had literally led him by the hand into his own bedroom and commenced undressing him. The moment was so insane and unlikely that he had found everything about it absolutely intriguing — from the fact that Gloria Wealdon was the only woman he had ever met who had to have a cigarette during love-making, to the fact that afterwards, as she bathed in his tub, she washed her panties in the bathwater along with the rest of her, and draped them over his faucet to dry.

"Tonight," she had said, "you're going to have dinner at 21 with a woman who isn't wearing any underpants."

During the second course at dinner, she leaned across her black bean soup and said, "Oh, kiddo, I'm still tingling there."

How on earth had it ever happened?

At times, he thought that some of the reason for it was that he felt sorry for her. She was so husky and red-cheeked and wholesome, looking like a member of the Radcliffe field hockey team, yet with that unbearable awkwardness about her, too, that was sometimes indigenous to her type woman — a clumsy shyness, helped wretchedly by the fact she was an upstate provincial.

"Oakey-doaky," she used to say, before Pitts taught her better.

"Hi, kiddo," she still said.

And, "Well, Paul Revere," which she sometimes said

upon leaving. It had taken Ralei a good month to realize that this was a pun on *au revoir*.

At other times he attributed his attraction to her (if it was an attraction) to her own sort of rustic aggressiveness. She was the only woman he had ever encountered who gave him the feeling that he was some form of shy and passive entity being wholly dominated by an aggressive force, a force somehow feminine. It was a decidedly pleasant feeling, despite the suspicion on Ralei's part that it was probably quite morbidly motivated. She was always directing things between them in physical matters: always yanking off the belt from his pants, or unzipping him so that the very sound of the act made him sometimes imagine that it was she unzipping her own fly, and he, trembling with a virgin's delight. She was forever saying, "Oh, look at you, P!" with sheer pleasure in her voice. "How beautiful you are!" so that he often felt quite conceited after one of their adventures.

Yet despite all this, and the fact that she was not really attractive as a woman (in fact, she was sometimes quite an embarrassment for Pitts), there was another flaw. He had seen it when she insisted on sending food back to the kitchen because something about it was not up to par, and he had seen it in her attitude toward the secretary he employed, toward clerks in stores, and a few times it had shown itself at cocktail parties they attended together, at luncheons with her publishers, at the booksellers' party. It was a stripe of unbelievable meanness, razor-sharp. It was the breath of life to her book, but Pitts had often met authors who wrote the worst kind of evil, yet were the gentlest, most retiring kind of men; at any rate, he had rarely seen their stripes, if indeed they had any. He had always thought that the cliché about authors writing out their hostilities and other emotions was somewhat true, that those who wrote murder books were thoroughly unequipped for any but the most bumbling kind of murder, and that historical romances were often enough written by schoolmarm types whom history would overlook and whom romance had already overlooked.

Gloria Wealdon, Pitts imagined, if she were not having an affair with you would undoubtedly be an extremely unpleasant person. Boring, impatient, and rude — the kind of person who prided herself on being outspoken and who never had anything to speak out about but the most unkind, impolite sort of backfence gossip.

Pitts glanced at his watch and decided not to be too early for his arrival in Cayuta. It would likely be a very delicate time, this time he would spend at the Wealdons'; delicate because Gloria would probably take no cares to look upon their situation as such, and while Milo Wealdon sounded quite like a creampuff, from all that Gloria said about him Pitts did not think he was the kind of man he would like to offend. Milo sounded not at all like a Milquetoast, but like that variety of male who is simply resigned to disaster (in this case his marriage) and whose bravest efforts are to retain some shred of dignity, some semblance of human communion — even at its minimal pitch — between himself and the woman he vowed to love, honor and obey. Such men were always of a gentle ilk; their wives, invariably, their opposite. That, of course, had to be their common ground, their raison d'être — their dissimilarity.

No, he would not arrive at Gloria Wealdon's early, as she had suggested. Pitts was certain he was not going to allow her to seduce him before dinner or after dinner, or at any time during the stay in Cayuta — and the very thought of it made him wish she were beside him, telling him to hurry up and find a side road, the way she often did on their drives together, telling him to hurry up, pulling his shirt tails out of his pants while he tried to keep the car on the road.

The thought made him extremely thirsty, and he pulled off the road at the next inn.

After the bartender placed the beer in front of him, Ralei found he had absolutely no money other than seven cents. He wrote out a check and presented it to the bartender, with his driving license. The check was one of his business ones, and the bartender studied it carefully.

He said, "What's this here, literary agent?"

"It's my business," said Pitts.

"Yeah? Whattaya do?"

"Sell books for authors to publishers."

"That's very interesting," said the bartender. "No kidding!"

Pitts decided to make a phone call and end the conversation. He wasn't particularly in the mood for any conversation, though ordinarily he found it quite pleasant to stop along the road and talk to barkeeps and the like. His mind was still on Gloria Wealdon, on the incredible physicality of her, and the equally incredible mentality. How she could be so attractive in one way, and so disenchanting in the other? He took the money from the barkeep and went back to give her a call. He would tell her he was on his way and perhaps invite her to join him at the hotel where he was staying in Cayuta. They could have a few drinks in the bar before they went to her house for dinner with her husband.

He received the number from the operator and it was busy.

He went back and worked over his beer.

After a while the bartender came wandering back to stand in front of him. "You see," he said, "we got this woman lives here that wrote a book."

"Here in the bar?"

"Naw," the bartender laughed. "Naw, here in Elbridge. That's the name of this place, mister."

"I didn't even know I was in a place. I thought I was between places."

"Most people don't know Elbridge is anything, 'less they live around here. We're not very big. Just the box and bag factory and this place and a gas station and a movie. They're all up ahead."

"Like a company town, hmmm?"

"Sort of a company town. The rest are farmers."

"And someone wrote a book about Elbridge?"

"No, not about Elbridge, mister, about Cayuta, New York, nearby here."

"Cayuta, New York?"

"Yeah. Same place that other book was about, you know, that one that's a big best seller now?"

"Population 12,360."

"That's right. That was written by someone from right over in Cayuta, New York."

"Yes, I know."

"You'd probably know all about that stuff, it being your business. I don't never pay any attention to that kind of stuff, you know? I don't do much reading. Got the television and business and everything. When I got free time, I go fishing. There's good fishing up around here. But this woman comes into the place all the time, and I got to talking about it."

"What woman?" said Pitts. "You mean Gloria Wealdon?"

"No, Miss Dare's her name. Edwina Dare. She lives here in Elbridge."

"And she wrote a book?"

"Yeah, about Cayuta. She used to live there, see? She worked in a bookstore there. Well, after a while she falls in love with this guy and he's married, you know? So things get pretty rough and the guy's tearing his hair out and he don't want his wife to know, and he's losing his business in the deal — got money problems."

Pitts made sympathetic noises, while the bartender

poured himself a shot of rum. "So," said the bartender, "he gets her a job up here."

"At the box and bag factory?" Pitts smiled.

"Yeah, but she's not like you might think. I mean she's no stupid factory girl. I gotta lot of them come in here and they're stupid, but this one's different. I even think she had a year at some college, you know? Somethin' musta happened like that, because she's not stupid like a lot of them. And he's okay himself."

"Who's *he?*"

"This guy from Cayuta's in love with her."

"Oh."

"Yeah, they carried on hot and heavy, you know? She's got this job, and she's staying at this place, boarding, and he's out to see her all the time. Got business with the box and bag company, you know? They're his suppliers or somethin', and it's all on the up and up, looks like. I mean, who around Elbridge even knows he's married? Course he has this kid, but — "

Pitts said, "But he doesn't bring the kid."

"Naw, he brings the kid, all right. Kid and Miss Dare get along peachy, you know? Think they were mother and daughter or somethin'. He brings the kid lots of times. Miss Dare says he always said he wasn't ashamed of her, he was proud of her, and he wanted his kid to know her. Well — " the bartender drank the rum in a gulp — "who's to know, you know? I wouldn't drag any kid of mine to meet the dame I was shackin up with, but that's what makes horse races, ain't it?"

"I guess it is."

"Kid used to be a little bit ah thing, first. Shot up overnight, seems — but it's been four, five years."

"That long, hmmm?"

"The lady used to run the boarding house where Miss Dare stayed died, and Miss Dare got left it. They was awful close, her and the lady. The lady wasn't ever married either, and I guess she had her romance or somethin' like that, because she took a shine to Miss Dare, and they were like mother and daughter. She left the place to her. Miss Dare kicked out all the boarders and lived there herself. Alone. And it was like that was his second home or something. Least once a week he was over here. More at times, but least once. Then she started fooling around."

"Fooling around?"

"With other men, you know? Used to burn him up. I'd hear him tell her she didn't have no right, and she'd tell him she couldn't help herself. Them were her exact words. She'd tell him she couldn't help herself. I'll marry you, he used to holler, Edwina, I'll marry you, but she'd always shake her head no and say she was already married, and she was Catholic. It was funny because you wouldn't expect it from a lady like her — class and everything. 'N she always called herself *Miss* Dare."

"I see," said Pitts.

"I mean, you'd think she'd be a Mrs. if she was married, and if she was one of them Catholics, you'd think — well, you wouldn't think she'd be that way. Every other way, nice, you know? Just had that wild streak. I dunno. And she doesn't look like no glamour doll either. Nice type."

"What's her book about?"

"About them, you know? Her and Mr. Fulton. About how they met and how they broke up, and how she come here, and *most* all the truth, you know? Only in her book she don't play around, and the guy she's in love with — Mr. Fulton — he dies on the road in an accident, on his way here. Oh, she don't call it Elbridge, and she don't call it Cayuta either, mind you, but it is Cayuta. Most of it's set there."

"You read the whole thing then?"

"I gotta admit it's a little too romantic for my tastes, you know? I like somethin' more for men. Adventure. But it's got some sexy stuff in it. Surprised the hell out of yours truly, mister!"

Pitts laughed.

The bartender said, "I mean, I knew there was these other men she was seeing behind his back, time to time, but you figure, hell, a woman's lonesome, and he's got his own place over in Cayuta, and why shouldn't she, you figure. You see, I'm no Catholic; I'm Methodist, only I don't go to church. But I figure her business is her business, don't you think that's the way to figure?"

"Yes," said Pitts. "Open me another beer, would you?"

"She's been pretty quiet lately, you know? Writing the book kept her occupied. Not that she was any lady of the night, either. Miss Dare can come in here any time of day or night and I'll be honored to serve her. But like she told Fulton, I guess sometimes she can't help it."

"I guess."

He grabbed a beer from the cooler under the bar. "Anyway, mister, that book she wrote is not to be read in church, you know? Not in the Catholic church and not in the Methodist church! It's got some hot stuff in it, know what I mean? And this doll is not the type, you'd think, but neither would you think she was shacked up all this time with some guy married to another woman, and herself Catholic and everything."

"Well," said Pitts, "that's interesting."

"Oh yes. Life is pretty interesting, mister. New York City ain't got a corner on sin."

"Where does this Miss Dare live? Nearby? I could leave my name with you, and she could write me a letter about her book. Don't tell her to send me the book. Just tell her to write me a letter about it, if she wants to."

Pitts decided that was a mistake the instant he said it. He had actually not meant to say it. He had just been sitting there thinking, Wouldn't it be fantastic; another woman from upstate New York with another exposé about the *same* town, and another best seller? He was even thinking about the press releases, about what could be made of it; but that was the way he always wasted time, with wonderful idle dreams while he was having a beer and letting his legs stretch — wonderful idle dreams about best sellers.

He chuckled. The bartender was pouring himself another shot of rum.

"Say, I'll tell her that," said the bartender. "What is it you do? You sell books?"

"I sell books to publishers. Not like a bookseller."

"Yeah? Well, she might just want to know all about you. I know she's anxious to meet that Mrs. Wealdon."

"Why?"

"Oh, you know. You want to meet someone who did it. I mean, get some tips. Miss Dare doesn't know what to do, and I can see the spot she's in. So you write a book, what next? You know?"

"I know."

"Her Mr. Fulton says she shouldn't see Gloria Wealdon. Well, he's not stupid, is he? I mean, a guy's not going to let his doll go blabber-mouthin' to Gloria Wealdon all about her book and what it's about. They had some big fight, I'll tell you! Boy!"

"Did she try to see Mrs. Wealdon?"

"Not yet. She was gonna, last week when she heard Mrs. Wealdon was comin' back from New York. He talked her out of it. Well, like she tole me, 'I'm not going to bare my soul to Gloria Wealdon,' she tole me, 'I just want to ask her advice about selling my book. It's selfish of him,' she tole me, 'he's just concerned with himself.' You see?" The bartender sighed. "Well, who knows? I don't blame the guy; I don't blame Miss Dare. But it's some mess. And now it's over, it's worse, you know? People try to be friends, but that's no good, you know?"

"What's over?" said Pitts.

"The affair. The affair's been over for about eight months

now, see? Oh, you know, they're friends and all, but the romance ain't been there. Not for about seven or eight months."

"So she wrote a book to make up for not having any romance any more."

"Say, you know," said the barkeep, "I never thought of it that way before, but that could be her story. You know?"

"I suppose so," said Pitts.

He got up and walked back to the phone booth, to try to get Gloria a second time. He decided not to encourage the bartender to give Miss Dare his name; yet while he decided it, he still felt intrigued by the idea that it would be wonderful and idiotic if Miss Dare had really written something he could sell; it would be delightful how it had all come about. Again, there was the busy signal. He told the operator not to call him back. He may as well go right on into Cayuta and call Gloria when he arrived at the hotel.

When he went back to the bar, the barkeep was grinning sheepishly.

"I suppose I done somethin' underhanded," he said.

"What do you mean?" said Pitts.

"Well," he said, "I called Miss Dare on my phone here. She don't live a stone's throw away. She's coming over," said the barkeep.

Seventeen

With all the tension coursing through the town, it was a wonder no murders had ever been committed there.
— FROM *Population 12,360*

The police sergeant had Gloria Wealdon's clipboard in his hand. He said, "Listen to this, will you? Just listen!"

The detective showed signs of impatience with the sergeant. He heaved a sigh and turned around in the room. Besides himself in the Wealdons' living room there were Min Stewart, Jay Mannerheim, Stanley Secora and Fern Fulton.

"Listen to what?" said the detective.

"Something here caught my eyes. I'll read it just the way it's written. Listen." He read the words very slowly and precisely: *"You don't fcare me Min, fo there!"*

Min Stewart said, "I'm not going to stay here any longer. What is anyone doing about Louie? Can you tell me that?"

"Steady," said Jay Mannerheim in a hushed voice. "I'm afraid there's nothing we can do. We'll have to stay here. But they'll continue to look for Louie. Don't worry."

In a corner, Stanley Secora sat slumped in a chair; the glasses he had recovered from the kitchen floor were steamed; his face was very white. Fern Fulton sat on the couch, wringing her handkerchief in her hands.

"Read that again," said the detective.

"You don't fcare me Min, fo there."

"Interesting," the detective said.

"She musta been drugged when she wrote it," said the sergeant, "that's why it's all confused. *Fo there,* for example. She could — "

"Oh, good God," said the detective.

"Well, how else could you explain it?"

"If a man's drunk, Carrington, it doesn't mean he spells his words the way he says them. His writing might be illegible, but he doesn't spell the words the way he says them, for Christ's sake."

Min Stewart shuddered at the cursing.

"Well, what could it mean?" said the sergeant.

"What could it mean, Mrs. Stewart?" the detective asked. "Would you know?"

"I have a lawyer for such matters," said Min Stewart.

"And I'm *very* concerned about my son!"

"So are we," the detective said. "We're concerned too."

"Then why would she write *fo* there?" said the sergeant.

"I don't know," the detective said. "Do you have any clues, Mrs. Stewart?"

"No."

"Want to tell us what you talked about at lunch with Mrs. Wealdon?"

"No."

"Why should she be scared of you, Mrs. Stewart?"

"Why should she be *fcared* of you, Mrs. Stewart?" the sergeant said.

"Yes," said the detective, "why *should* she be fcared?"

Min Stewart said nothing.

The detective motioned to the sergeant, and they went into the bedroom.

"I'll leave here with the lovely lady," said the detective, indicating the dead body of Gloria Wealdon still on the bed, "but the chief wants you to keep them here until he arrives."

"He's going to question them here?"

"Yes."

"What's that?" said the sergeant.

On the floor there was the broken globe, and the figure of a saint.

"Soap," the detective said. "Somebody carved something out of soap."

"Looks like a nun. They Catholics?"

"Don't let it influence you either way, Carrington," the detective said facetiously. "Secora must have knocked this over when he ran out of here."

"Since when have I been partial to Catholics?"

"Just don't start now."

"They aren't Catholics," the sergeant said. "I never heard that."

"I'm going to leave Secora's statement with you, and

you can give it to the chief. It won't do him much good now, because I took it down in shorthand, but it'll be useful later when he wants to compare his statement with the one I got while Secora was still shaking."

"What do you think of it?" the sergeant said. "How about that Min Stewart?"

"Christ, Carrington, it could be practically anyone in the town, couldn't it? Who the hell liked her after that lousy book?"

"I don't think it's anybody here," said the sergeant

"I'll keep that in mind," the detective said. "Blockhead!" He began to laugh. "I never heard such a blockhead state-ment as *fcare* and *fo* being proof Gloria Wealdon was drugged when she wrote her notes. You're a dilly, Sergeant, a real dilly!"

"You got to hand it to me, it doesn't make any sense her spelling words that way."

"I got to hand it to you," said the detective, placing the soap sculpture in the sergeant's hand. "Here, and don't get your fingerprints on it, sweetheart, because I won't alibi you. I think you probably did it, anyway. Didn't she have a mean cop in that book? Or a stupid one?"

"She didn't have any cops in it," said the sergeant. "That's what was wrong with it."

"C'mon," the detective said. "It stinks in here."

While the detective and the sergeant were out of the room, Fern Fulton went across and knelt by Min Stewart's side.

"Where'd Freddy go, Min?"

"I think he went to find Virginia, dear. Don't worry."

"Fern," said Mannerheim, "just relax now. Just take it easy."

"Glo's dead," Fern said again. Her face wrinkled up again in that peculiar way of a woman's crying. "Oh migod, I don't know what to think any more. I don't know what to think about anything. I know something's terribly, terribly wrong."

"It'll be all right soon," said Min Stewart. "Freddy will be back and it'll be all right soon."

"Go sit down, Fern," said Mannerheim. He helped her to her feet and across the room.

Secora looked at him. He said, "I didn't do it, Doctor. I swear, I just came across her body like that. I didn't do it. I just f-f-f-fow-ond," and he began to cry again too; the deep, inside sobbing.

Jay went back and sat beside Min Stewart.

"I think he's still in this house," said Min.

"Shhh, Min, easy now. You won't do yourself any good."

"I do. They never searched. Isn't it peculiar that they never searched, Jay?"

"Yes, I suppose it is. I don't think we've ever had a murder in Cayuta. They're probably very uncertain about procedure."

"At least not one anyone's ever known about."

"What do you mean?"

"I mean at least Cayuta has not had a murder anyone knows about."

"Hmmm? Oh, yes, yes," said Jay, barely able to smile. "Yes, of course."

"I just have the idea he's very close by, Jay. I know my son."

"Well, if he is — "

"What?"

"I don't know," he said frankly.

"You see."

"Min, I'm not at all convinced Louie did this."

"Aren't you?"

"No, I'm not. I've never thought of Louie as homicidal at all. Suicidal maybe, but not — "

"Oh. Jay, really, who knows *who* is a homicidal type? If

anyone were able to tell that surely, why wouldn't we have fewer homicides? No, Jay, the mind can't tell you everything, but sometimes the heart can tell you what the mind isn't able to."

"And your heart told you Louie did this?"

"I don't want to think that, but ..."

"Then don't."

"He's schizophrenic, you say."

"Yes, a catatonic."

"She should have listened to me."

"It's too late to ponder over what Gloria Wealdon should or should not have done now. And it's too early to imagine you know what Louie could or couldn't do. Min, schizophrenia is the psychotic reaction par excellence. It's the most complicated, mysterious mental disease we have; we don't know very much at all about it."

"Do you agree he could have gotten here in time to kill her?"

"I think he *could* have."

"Then don't tell me anything more."

"Lord, Min, we don't even know how she died."

"She was poisoned probably. They always throw up, I should imagine."

"But a person can throw up for many reasons, Min. She could have been choked, or shot, anything...."

"Louie'd poison her, I think."

"You're just torturing yourself," said Jay Mannerheim.

When the detective and the sergeant came from the other room, Fern Fulton said, "What is anyone doing about my daughter, my husband?"

"We're looking for them, Mrs. Fulton. Both of them, particularly him."

"You don't think Freddy ..."

"He was here," said the sergeant. "He was here and he left, and we'd like to have a word with him, if that doesn't put him to too much trouble."

"Freddy wouldn't kill a fly," said Fern Fulton.

"Mrs. Wealdon wasn't a fly," the sergeant said.

Oddly, Stanley Secora stopped crying long enough to giggle; then he began sobbing again.

"I'm going to have a look around the house," the detective said. "Might as well while I'm waiting."

"It's a publicity stunt," said Fern Fulton. "I don't believe she's dead."

"You want to have a look, m'am?" said the sergeant.

"No."

"Then kindly keep still about publicity stunts."

The detective was rummaging around, opening and closing doors in the house.

Min whispered to Jay, "Now, they'll find him."

"You think your son's here, Mrs. Stewart?" said the sergeant.

"He *could* be here."

"I wonder what he'd be doing here?"

"We none of us exactly planned this gathering," said Min.

"No, we none of us did." The sergeant looked suspiciously at her. "We none of us did, did we, m'am!"

After a few moments, the ambulance from the Cayuta hospital came, and with it the county coroner, the chief of police, an intern and half a dozen neighborhood boys of all sizes and shapes chasing after them. The chief of police told them they would all be arrested if they did not get away from the Wealdon house, but they stayed in a little knot out front, unmoving, knowing that, whatever it was inside, it was really serious, and that the chief of police would not carry through his threat, because something had happened inside the house that was very, very bad....
What? They scratched their elbows and their legs and leaned against one another, watching the house.

The men all marched into the Wealdons' solemnly, and

all but the chief of police went into the bedroom.

The chief of police smiled. "Howdy?" he said.

Jay Mannerheim said hello back, but no one else said anything. The chief of police looked embarrassed.

He said, "I guess we got some trouble on our hands. You folks don't mind cooperating with me, I hope. I'm going to have to keep you here, so if you want to call your loved ones, you can."

He used the phrase "your loved ones" only when things were serious; but, really, things had never been this serious; a few killings in the migrant camps nearby, but never the murder of a respectable woman. At least, she was supposed to be respectable. Never mind she wrote dirty books — that wasn't the business of the police department.

The chief of police was on his way into the bedroom when the detective appeared at the top of the basement stairs and called out: "I need some help here. I've found someone."

Min Stewart stiffened. "Oh, Jay," she said. "Jay, here it comes. I must steel myself now."

"She scratches like a little tom-cat," said the detective.

The sergeant and the detective helped the struggling girl into the living room.

Fern Fulton ran to her daughter, nearly hysterical.

"She was hiding in the basement," said the detective. "Secora, let her sit where you are."

Stanley Secora crossed the room to the side where Jay sat with Min Stewart. "Don't push her," he said to the sergeant, and then clapped his hand over his mouth. "I mean — "

"We're not pushing her," the sergeant said. "She won't stop kicking."

"Virginia!" said Mrs. Fulton. "Oh, Virginia!"

The pair fell in the chair together and embraced, both weeping, the girl with her face buried in her mother's bosom.

They were bringing the body out now, down the steps of the split level, through the foyer to the hall.

They were opening the screen door, and working the stretcher out to the sidewalk.

"There's a sheet over the face," said a young boy's voice. "Someone's dead."

Eighteen

Many people think that love is two-toned, if not multi-colored, but love is one color only, and that color is red. Red! red! red! — whirling before your eyes bright as a poppy, commanding as a traffic light, only you do not stop for the color of love — you go, you forget all the rules and just go!
— FROM *Population 12,360*

Freddy Fulton drove South on Route 2.

In half an hour he would reach Elbridge. He was sure he would find Virginia there with Edwina, but now a new thought bothered him. What was happening to Edwina? What was happening to change her so remarkably, now, near the end of everything between them?

This thought overshadowed the fear of Edwina's going to Gloria for help with her novel. *(Help.* Freddy wanted to laugh. Edwina would tell Gloria the whole business in an eye's wink; she wouldn't *ask* Gloria Wealdon anything. All she'd been doing since their affair came to an end was tell people about it. Anyone — the bartender at the Elbridge Inn, a stranger, one of her men, anyone — just tell people. Pound it out on the typewriter and blab it out all over the place, but tell, tell, tell!) It had not been easy for Freddy Fulton to make the decision to sever his relationship with Edwina.

One would imagine it was the easiest thing in the world

for a man to do — break up with someone who was not his wife and who had not even been faithful to him as a mistress. It should have been easy, too, by all logic and reason; he should have been able simply to say, "It's all over now, Edwina; I've had enough. I don't want you any more." Another man, maybe any other man in the world but Freddy Fulton, would have been quite glib about coming to such a decision, but Freddy Fulton was the only man who loved Edwina Dare. That was the difference.

Freddy supposed, too, that it was just another of life's infinite ironies that Edwina Dare was not even a beautiful woman. He guessed she did not even have that casual kind of prettiness that made men turn and look at a woman on the street and wonder what it would be like to have her in bed. She was simply a woman he had very slowly fallen in love with, a woman who had begun by helping him order books on plant management down at The Book Mart in Cayuta, and who had ended by capturing him so completely and thoroughly in every possible connotation of the word that he was ready to divorce Fern for her and give up Virginia. But she would not even allow this — her religion, she said (only she called it "my faith") — and it never seemed to make any difference to her that she was his mistress and not his wife, because her "faith" did not believe in divorce. She had married, she told him, when she was very young; and her husband had left her because she was unfaithful. She had never pulled any punches, never tried to pretend that her husband was unfaithful or that something else had gone wrong; she had simply told him straight out.

When he tried to think what it was he loved about her, he was like many men: he either had to enlarge on her good qualities or tell himself he simply didn't care what it was he loved about her; he just loved her, and he loved loving her, and that was all there was to it. But there were

THE GIRL ON THE BEST SELLER LIST

some things he could speak about — feelings, really, and sketchy ways of hers: the easy sound of soft laughter, husky voice inflections, the funny-sweet way she said his name, Fre-ad, as though it were two syllables. She wore her hair brushed up above her temples, and a vein throbbed there when she was tired. He knew the sudden way she would lean forward when she was excited, though her voice stayed always low. She read poetry. Sometimes, if she didn't like a certain tie on him, she asked him not to wear it again because it wasn't right for him; and she told him what colors she loved on him. He could talk and talk and talk to her, and she always listened, as though it was the most interesting thing she had ever heard; she always listened that way, even if he was talking about something that had happened at the plant, something not really important at all.

Whatever it was about her, Freddy Fulton loved it, and he loved her probably more than he had ever loved any woman in his life. His decision to end their affair was due partly to her inability to be faithful to him and partly to his own inability to reconcile a love for this sort of woman with his love for his daughter and Fern. She used to tell him that the "other men" didn't matter to her, and he somehow believed that, or knew it, or sensed it. Whatever it was, he knew she loved him, but he knew also that she had in her an inability to prove her love for him by not seeing others. Her "faith" was a convenient dodge. She would never let herself be wholly tied down to any man.

Freddy had always thought that women like that were either wild ones who drank and caroused and cracked bad jokes with the boys, or else decadent-looking types who were nervous as cats and interested in very little in the world. But Edwina Dare was neither of these. She was an enigma.

"You're all I have, Fre-ad," she had said when he told her about his decision. And he knew what she meant —

that he was the only one whom she had ever loved and approximated a marriage with; the only one — and what a marriage! One where the husband was not home nights, or mornings, but maybe once or twice a week. One where each shared almost everything the other thought, but not a house and not a family and, most of the time, not even the same bed overnight. In a way, they shared Virginia, and Freddy was not sorry that he had let Edwina and her become close friends; but Virginia knew as well as he did that there was something unwholesome about Edwina and himself — unwholesome, and yet so right when they were together that it literally brought tears to his eyes near the end, when he was making his decision.

She had taken it bravely, but not wisely. In a way, he was pleased that she had not taken it wisely; pleased because her helter-skelter plans and ideas for the future showed her in such a vulnerable light, a light that reflected the terrible intensity of their love for one another. It was a selfish pleasure that somehow relieved a bit his own pain at the thought of their separation. Her idea to write the book seemed to him so idiotic that at times it made him laugh aloud, and at times it broke his heart to think of her having such an idea.

Now, the book was written; and now, this change had come over her: this certain brazenness, as though she would not leave Elbridge or the vicinity of Cayuta without having left her mark. Why? Freddy could answer that question. It wasn't anything that had gotten into Edwina; it was something that had gone out of her; it was the final dying of love, and with it the empty aftermath that had to be filled. There was no way to fill it; no children of their love, no home (just the old boarding house Mrs. Devrow left her, with memories of other men there, too); nothing but the same old job at the box and bag factory in that dizzy little upstate town she'd had reason to live in for five years, and then ... the Future, a blank. The Future, and she must be very scared suddenly of that.

Freddy pulled the sun blind down on the Buick's windshield and frowned as he drove. No, he should not blame Edwina, or wonder at what had come over her. He knew she was spiteful and angry and even bent on revenge of some sort, and he knew she was ashamed of it because he didn't deserve it; she was bitterly ashamed of everything she had done to him, ashamed of herself and sorry for herself. So this was the way she showed her spite and her anger; and the ways by which she sought her revenge were unconsciously over-blown ways.

The book she wrote. What did she call it? *Goodbye to Yesterday.* In the book, she had made him run off the road in his automobile. Killed him off, in other words.

Freddy felt a sick wave of nostalgia flood through him, remembering back on all the days and nights they had had which were sweet and very dear and then thinking of Edwina sitting up at night writing that book, writing how he had lost control at the wheel, writing how the car had spun, how he had screamed — writing, killing him off. That was one of her over-blown ways of getting even, without even really knowing it.

"Do you like the book?" she had asked.

"Why kill your hero?" he had said.

"I couldn't think of any other way to end it."

Freddy thought maybe that was the truth; maybe that was the only way she would ever be able truly to think of it as over. Even though neither of them felt anything physically any more, and even though that horrendous proof was sufficient reason for both to know that the affair was ended, probably Edwina would never accept it until he *was* dead. Women never let go, unless they are married to you; then they let go too soon. Was that right?

Another way she was getting even was with sudden dramatics. It wasn't like Edwina ever to call him at home on a Saturday, to threaten him that way, to announce that if he did not arrange to bring Gloria Wealdon to her, she would go to Gloria Wealdon, that very evening. They had agreed, early in the game, never to abuse their code, never to make an Elbridge call anywhere except from a phone booth to a phone booth. After Edwina took over Mrs. Devrow's, he called her there directly, but Edwina was not ever supposed to call him at home. Only in an emergency. In the past few months she had become sloppy about this. She had pretended to be someone at the box and bag factory, sometimes even speaking directly with Fern, asking for him, as she did this noon when she had called. He had stood there with Fern not a few feet away, while she said, "I'm serious, Fred. I have to see Gloria Wealdon. The only way for me is to sell my book and go and live in New York."

He had hurried to his office after lunch, and told her by telephone that he would send her to New York. "That's the way to do it," he said. "Get some place to live there. Look for a job, taking your time, of course," he had added generously, "and send your book around to the various publishers."

"I can't just go there cold. I can't do that."

"I'll come and see you tomorrow," he had promised.

Well, tomorrow wasn't soon enough after all, and that was his fault too. At lunch he had told Virginia about her call. She'd known about Edwina's threats to call on Gloria — they had even laughed a little about them together — but lately Virginia had been more and more concerned about the possibility of Fern's ever finding out about the Edwina thing.

"You know, we've both been unfaithful to her in a sense," she had said one day. "Poor Mother. I feel quite bad about it, for my part. I should have kept out of it."

"I should have kept you out of it," he said.

"It wasn't your fault. I was as much to blame."

"You grew up knowing Edwina. Virginia, in some ways

you even acquired some of her mannerisms. I believe that at times you're actually quite alike."

"More than mother and I are, I think."

"I think so too."

"But do you know something, Father, I not only love Mother better, I respect her more. Why is that?"

"I guess it's because you really think of your mother as being good, because she wasn't an unfaithful woman, and you think of Edwina as bad."

"I suppose there's something to that."

"Yes," Freddy said.

"And in a way, I suppose I'm glad that Edwina's trying to go to New York to live."

Freddy said, "Yes, and so am I."

He was afraid now, though, of something he had never really thought about much. While everything was up in the air the way it was, with Edwina still in Elbridge and still ambitious for her novel, how might she hurt Virginia? For surely Virginia was what he loved most, and surely that would eventually dawn on Edwina Dare. He was afraid of that, and being afraid of it, he drove all the faster along Route 2.

As he went racing along, he wished that he had been able to locate Milo before he had set off for Elbridge. He had driven to the high school to find him, to tell him that Gloria might need him (no sense saying more than that; the good Lord knows Min *could* be wrong about Louie). But Milo wasn't there. No one seemed to know where he was. Nearly everyone said that it was most peculiar, because he almost never missed a Saturday meet.

When Freddy Fulton heard the police siren, he damned himself for forgetting the speed trap between Elbridge and the county line. He saw the troopers on the motorcycles behind him, and he laughed to think that both men behind the billboard where they set the trap had whipped out after him. He pulled over to the side and lit a cigarette, waiting for one of them to come back and ticket him. When they both came back, he chuckled. "Hey, fellows," he said. "Take it easy. I'm not dangerous."

"Maybe you're not," said one of them, "but your license plate number came over our radio a while back."

"Mine?"

"You're wanted back in Cayuta, Mr. Fulton," the other one said, opening the door and getting in beside Freddy Fulton. "Suspicion of murder."

Nineteen

"I love surprises," Gina said. "I don't care what it is, I love to be surprised. I hope I die surprised!"
— FROM *Population 12,360*

At five-ten, Sergeant Carrington stood in the kitchen studying the stack of dirty dishes in the sink with an expressionless face. At the dinette, the chief of police was talking with Virginia Fulton.

"... because it's very serious," he was saying, "and we have to know everything."

"Even her name?"

"Everything."

"Edwina Dare," she said. "She was my father's mistress."

"And why didn't you want her to speak with Mrs. Wealdon?"

"Because she'd tell her everything!"

"And why didn't you want Mrs. Wealdon to know?"

"Because Mrs. Wealdon was mean. She'd tell my mother."

"So why had you come here this afternoon?"

"I was going to ask Mrs. Wealdon not to see her."

"Ask her? If she was mean, she wouldn't listen to you,

would she?"

"N-no."

"Well, then! What about it?"

"All right, I was going to threaten her."

"How?"

"I didn't have any real plan. It was an impulsive thing. I was just going to try and scare her."

"And what did you do?"

"I hid in her closet. I got in through the cellar door, and I hid up in her bedroom closet."

"Why did you hide like that?"

"I wanted to scare her."

"Then what?"

"I — waited until she came home and into the bedroom. She was throwing something into the closet — a girdle and some shoes or something, it's all very unclear — but I hadn't expected her to whip the door open like that. I'd wanted to jump out at her, not to have her surprise me."

"Then what?"

"She said, 'Why you little brat! What do you want?'"

"Then?"

"She said, 'Just what in hell are you doing in my closet, you ...'"

"What?"

"She called me a cross-eyed brat."

"And what did you do?"

"I picked up a coat hanger. I don't know why. I was all worked up. I picked up a coat hanger and I hit her."

"Where?"

"Across her back. I didn't think."

"Don't cry any more now."

"I'll try not to."

"What then?"

"She tried to catch hold of the hanger and get it out of my hand. She chased me around the room. I remember I knocked over the globe there with the soap sculpture inside it. She said, 'Now, you've done it. I've had that thing for years!' She was yelling at me and chasing me."

"Had you hit her again?"

"No."

"Then?"

"Then I heard her moan. It was a funny sound she made. I turned around and she was running the other way, running toward the bathroom. I stood still and watched her. She went inside and I heard her vomiting. I didn't know what to do. I just stood there, and then I remember that she came out. She was holding her stomach. Her face was a very funny color, nearly purple. She looked off in the distance as though she couldn't see out of her eyes. It was as though I wasn't there at all."

"Then?"

"She fell on the bed. She was gasping for breath. I said, 'Mrs. Wealdon, what's the matter with you?' but I don't believe she could hear me."

"Then?"

"I ran to the telephone. I was going to call Doctor Mannerheim. I had wanted to call him last week and tell him that I was afraid Edwina would tell Mrs. Wealdon, and that it would get back to my mother and just crack her up." The girl began to cry, sobs forcing her body to heave. The sergeant walked from the kitchen to the door of the living room, while the police chief patted her hair. "There now, Virginia," he said, "try to finish. Then you can rest."

"I couldn't have done that with a hanger, could I? I'm not that strong." She was sobbing again, uncontrollably.

"You'll just have to try, Virginia," said the policeman. "What happened then? Did you call the doctor?"

"Almost, but then I remembered that he wasn't a real doctor, that he wouldn't be able to help her. She was really too sick; she needed a real doctor, maybe even the hospital. I was going to call to the operator that it was an emergency. I should have done that, I know that."

"Why didn't you?"

"The doorbell began ringing. I was deathly afraid. Mrs. Wealdon was just barely making breathing sounds there on the bed, and she was sick again, but she couldn't move. I was too afraid to do anything but get away. I ran to the back stairs that go to the basement. I was going to run out the door and down through the fields, but when I looked out the door I saw Stanley Secora coming in the back way. I shut the door and stayed in the basement. I was numb by then, I was so scared."

"Were you afraid of being blamed for her death?"

"I was afraid of death, that's all."

"What do you mean, Virginia?"

"I mean, I'd never seen anything like that. Just nothing. I was never in such a situation in all my life, don't you understand?"

"I think so."

"It was like a nightmare. I knew Stanley Secora was breaking into the Wealdons', and I knew Gloria Wealdon was dying up in the bedroom, and I'd hit her, and I was in the basement — but none of this seemed logical or real to me. I just began to shake, and I felt as though I were perhaps dead myself, or dreaming. I don't know — "

"Then?"

"Always then! Oh, listen, I didn't mean to hit her! I never even planned to hit her!"

"Virginia, be calm."

The sergeant wandered into the living room. Fern Fulton sat in the deep chair, staring out at the twilight, biting her knuckles. In the corner opposite, Min Stewart was speaking with Secora, and Jay Mannerheim was resting his head by holding his hand to it, covering his eyes, his elbow balanced on his knee.

At the sound of the telephone, everyone became alert. The sergeant answered it.

He seemed to say little else than "Yes. Yes. Okay. Right. Yes."

Then he hung up.

"Anything?" said the voice of the chief of police from the other room.

The sergeant went inside and they spoke in hushed voices together. When he returned to the living room, he said, "I got three news flashes."

"Well?" said Min Stewart.

"Well," said the sergeant, "number one is she was poisoned. That's how she got it."

"And the rest?" said Min Stewart.

"Number two is we picked up Mr. Fulton. He'll be along here soon."

Mrs. Fulton didn't answer. She just put the handkerchief to her eyes again.

"And now comes number three," the sergeant said. "Number three is we picked up Louis Stewart, Jr. He was in the five-and-ten," said the sergeant, "stealing."

"He was what?" said Min Stewart.

"He was at the dinnerware counter, m'am, stealing spoons."

Twenty

Someday, Gina thought, Will will be a man to contend with.
— FROM *Population 12,360*

The police surgeon said, "It all checks out, Dave."

"In your mind maybe," said the chief of police, "but I don't get it."

"You want to explain it, Jay?" said the police surgeon. "I can take the Stewart kid along to the Retreat."

"Just tell me one thing," said the chief of police, "what

the devil was he stealing spoons for? What's that got to do with all of this?"

"*That,*" said the police surgeon, "hasn't got *anything* to do with this. That's the beauty of the catatonic mind — it just isn't predictable. One might decide to throw popcorn at a bus, and another might decide to axe his great aunt. *Louie* stole spoons. Simple."

Louie Stewart sat on the bench in the detention room, head hanging, eyes glassy, looking at nothing, hands limp.

The chief of police shook his head. "Okay, Jay," he said. "You might as well take over."

"Before I do, I think someone ought to stop by at the Fultons' later. It was a shock for the little girl."

"Her mother, too," said the chief of police. "I wouldn't like to be Freddy Fulton tonight."

"It's not my business," said the police surgeon. "Maybe their family doctor … maybe they're just better left alone."

"Maybe you're right," said Jay. "Anyway, I'll give them a call before I leave here."

The police surgeon went over to Louie Stewart and reached down to take his arm. "C'mon, fellow."

Louie didn't even look up.

"C'mon," said the police surgeon. He pulled him up, and Louie did not resist. The pair left the room, Louie shuffling along with a dazed expression to his face while the police surgeon propelled him.

"I guess we have Louie's mother to thank for solving this thing," said Mannerheim.

"Do you want to start from the beginning?" said the police chief.

Mannerheim nodded. "The name of the poison is cantharidin," he began. "The doctor explained that it's derived from a species of beetle. In its crystallized form, it's a very violent irritant. It causes blisters if you handle it."

"Is that how she spotted it?"

"Yes. Min Stewart probably knows as much about pharmaceuticals as her husband did. You know how sharp she is."

"A hawk."

"Yes. Well, she was sitting beside Secora at the Wealdons'. His hands were bandaged, but one of the bandages was coming undone. She saw the blisters and she began to put two and two together."

"When I got there," said the police chief, "she thought her son did it."

"I know. I guess she sensed Louie was cracking up, and she was afraid the kid would kill. I never thought he was a killer."

"I wish I knew why everyone always calls him a kid."

"He's not a kid," said Mannerheim, "that's true. But you couldn't call him a man. Anyway — "

"Yes, let's get it over with."

"Min noticed Secora's hands. This was just after the phone call came about Louie being found. Min got me off in a corner and told me she was suspicious about Stanley's burns. I didn't pay much attention. He'd told me himself, earlier, that he'd burned his hands, and he's so clumsy I just didn't think there was much basis for her suspicions. Besides, she'd been telling me over and over that Louie poisoned Gloria Wealdon. So when she told me Stanley did it, I just figured Min was getting a little hysterical."

"But you talked to Stanley then?"

"Yes. You were still questioning Virginia Fulton in the kitchen, and Sergeant Carrington, well — "

"He wasn't very happy," said the chief of police. "He was supposed to have the afternoon off."

"Yes," Mannerheim nodded. "So I just casually got into conversation with Stanley. I went over and sat by him, and we just began talking. When I asked him how he hurt his hands, he began to blush. He said he'd burned them making candy for Mrs. Wealdon. Then *I* began to get suspicious, particularly when he told me he made only two pieces of candy for her."

"You're sure about that?"

"Oh, yes. There were only two." Jay said. "One of them had only the very slightest amount of cantharidin. The medical examiner says Stanley told him there was no more than one two-hundredths of a grain in that piece. And that's borne out by the vial he produced, and the emergency autopsy. Mrs. Wealdon got the second piece, the one Stanley really slugged. About three grains' worth was in that piece."

"Then the first piece is still missing?"

"She may or may not have eaten that one, too. That's not important. It wouldn't do any damage to anyone, not concrete damage. Stanley had intended to eat that piece himself."

"But I still don't get it!" said the chief of police. "What did Secora have against Gloria Wealdon? *He* wasn't in her book, was he?"

"That's the peculiar part," Jay Mannerheim answered. "I didn't read the book carefully, so I can't say. But Secora claimed there was an odd-jobs character in the novel, one to whom the heroine was very attracted. He was a character named Will, I think. Secora used to help Milo around their place — cut lawns, plant things — you know what a jack-of-all-trades he is. Secora got the idea he was Will in her novel, and he reasoned that she must be attracted to him. Apparently the heroine was afraid to 'let herself go' with this Will character, but she was always daydreaming about him. Well," Jay shrugged and smiled sadly, "that's who Secora thought he was: Will. He figured Gloria Wealdon was the heroine and he was Will."

"That's a reason to *kill?*" said the police officer.

"Stanley didn't want to kill her, Dave. You see, he had an appointment with her. He thought he was going to spend the afternoon with her alone. Milo would be at the track meet, he thought, and he'd be alone with Mrs. Wealdon. Stanley wanted to make love to her."

"He what?"

"And it *could* have worked — *if* she'd kept the appointment, and *if* she'd taken the candy with the small dose. Cantharidin, in a tiny dose, acts as an aphrodisiac."

"Wait a minute — why the *two* pieces?"

"That's the flaw, Dave. Stanley had no way of knowing, or let's say no way of comprehending, that cantharidin is a deadly poison. He knew it was an aphrodisiac, and his plan was to give himself just a pinch for a push, and to really slug hers. He had the pieces marked. There was an almond on the piece he intended for himself. What would have happened, probably, would be very nearly the same as what did happen. Gloria Wealdon would have eaten the piece without the almond, and died right before his eyes."

"But you said she didn't keep her appointment."

"She didn't. But she accepted the candy from him, and he was too nervous and flustered to think what to do. So he simply decided that he would return to her house after she got back from lunch, and try again. The worst Stanley could imagine was that she might have eaten the candy before he got there, and by the time he got there, the effect he'd intended might have worn off."

"Where the hell did he get the stuff?"

"He's a loader for Fulton Pharmaceutical Supply. Apparently in the army he'd heard about this cantharidin. He told me all he knew was that it made women 'hot.' Even when he burned his hands, he didn't figure out that it was poison. He said he thought he might be allergic to it, said his skin was sensitive to a lot of things. He had plenty of things wrong with him when he came back after the war, you know that. I don't think he's been right since."

"So he just thought it was something else like that?"

"Yes. He said that was another reason he put so little in his own piece. He said he thought he might be sensitive to it, the way he is to Vitamin C."

"Oh, Jesus!" said the chief of police. *"This* takes the cake!"

"I know. For a while there this afternoon I actually thought Freddy Fulton's kid did it."

"It could have been anybody," said the officer, "there were so many people in town who hated her!"

"But love killed her," Jay said, "and there weren't that many in Cayuta who loved her."

The police officer sighed. Then he said, "By the way, has anyone located Milo Wealdon yet?"

"Not that I know of."

"I've got Lieutenant Kelly up at the Wealdons' place in case Milo comes home, but it's damn strange he can't be located, wouldn't you say?"

"It is," said Jay. "I thought he might have done it, too, earlier."

Jay picked up his suitcoat and his hat from the chair. "I have to run along now, Dave. I'll give the Fultons a call, and if everything's all right there I think I'll go home."

"I don't see how everything could be all right there."

"You'd be surprised," said Jay. "People are funny. In a crisis, you can suddenly accept an awful lot you'd never be able to accept under normal circumstances. In a way, it's a lucky thing Fern Fulton found out about her husband's affair right at this time. On an ordinary day, she might have cracked up."

"It's tough about Min Stewart's kid. I guess Gloria Wealdon can really chalk one up there. *Could* have, I mean."

"She just triggered it. It was on its way; it would have happened eventually."

The police officer said, "Well, I guess we can call it a day now. Some day, huh, Jay!"

"Some day!" Jay Mannerheim agreed.

As he turned to leave the detention room, the officer called him.

"Before you go, Jay, do you mind spelling the name of that poison for me?"

"C-a-n-t-h-a-r-i-d-i-n," Jay Mannerheim said. "That's the technical name. It's in the report. Most people don't call it that," he added. "Most people call it Spanish-fly."

Twenty-one

Goodbye to that town, and good riddance too!
— THE END OF *Population 12,360*

Pitts Ralei drove North on Route 2.

"I'm afraid you've made me very late," he said.

"Do you regret it?"

"No, but …"

"But what?"

"I have to stop and try Mrs. Wealdon's number again."

"Now she's *Mrs.* Wealdon."

"Well — "

"Well, will I be *Miss* Dare one day?"

"Edwina — "

"Will I?"

"You're making me extremely nervous and I don't know these roads."

"I know them. Oh, how I know them!"

"Do you have to bring it up?"

"Does it make you jealous, Pitts? I hope it does."

"What's that?"

"What?"

"That thing around your neck that keeps clinking."

"It's a medal."

"Oh, are you religious?"

"I have my faith…. It's a medal of St. John Port Latin. I got it for bravery."

"I never should have had that last Martini. I never

should have had the first one. Beer and Martinis!"

"Now you're starting to regret everything. In a minute you'll tell me to get out and walk."

"No, I won't tell you that. But remember, you'll have to stay at the hotel while I dine with the Wealdons."

"I don't mind that. I don't need her help now."

"You can rest and sleep. I won't stay there long."

"Then you'll come back to me, won't you?"

"Yes."

"You'll have a horrible time anyway. Milo Wealdon is a terrible bore."

"So I've heard."

"He made me so nervous. He called me Edwin. I felt like a man when he called me Edwin."

"Did he know about you and Fulton?"

"Sometimes I think he guessed. I think so."

"We have to stop while I call Gloria. You watch for a place."

"Pitts."

"What?"

"Do you think you can sell my book?"

"I've only read a few pages. I don't know. It sounds good, but I don't want to build your hopes up until I'm sure."

"But you will let me drive to New York with you? You will help me?"

"Yes," said Ralei. "Yes."

"I'll listen to any suggestions you make about the book. I'm not afraid to take criticism."

"They all say that."

"But I'm really not!"

"I remember how hard it was to get Gloria to make a change."

"Oh, her!"

"Her characters were really quite hard."

"I don't wonder."

"Do you remember the book well?"

"Yes."

"Do you remember Will?"

"He was the sexiest man in it."

"He was my idea."

"That doesn't surprise me."

"No, seriously now. Listen to me, and sit back, for heaven's sake! I mean it about these roads. They wind."

"All right, Pittsy. I'll sit back."

"I don't know what it is about you upstate women, but you're certainly a breed apart."

"Why do you say that?"

"Never mind. Let's get back to Will."

"Ah, Will, handsome, virile, wonderful Will, with the grass in the cuffs of his pants."

"Yes. She fought it, you know. She didn't want her heroine to be attracted to an odd-jobs man. Her heroine was a very cold character."

"And you changed all that."

"Yes, I did. The heroine needed softening. She needed some character about whom she felt something more than disgust, or pity, or hatred."

"Desire!"

"Yes."

"You'll find plenty of desire in my book."

"It isn't a bitter book, then?"

"No. I'm not bitter about Freddy."

"Good."

"There's a place you can call from, Pitts, there on the right."

Pitts swung the Sunbeam Talbot into the gasoline station, coming to an abrupt, noisy stop.

"I'll wait for you," she said, "but hurry."

As he walked toward the phone booth, he had ample proof that he never should have had the last Martini. He was very definitely swaying.

Ten minutes later, when Pitts Ralei came out of the phone booth, his face was ashen. He got into the car and started the motor.

"Where's the nearest bar and restaurant?" he said.

"What?"

"I said where's the nearest bar and restaurant?"

"About a mile before we reach Cayuta."

"You're hungry, aren't you?"

"Well, I can eat, if that's what you mean. But what about Gloria Wealdon?"

"Something's come up," he said. "I'm not sure we want to barge in on Mrs. Wealdon just now."

"I don't understand you."

"I know you don't. Let's just drop it. Let's find somewhere we can get a drink."

"Whatever you say," Edwina Dare said uncertainly.

Over dinner, after a few drinks, Pitts would tell her. It would not matter much to her, probably. In a sense, it was himself he would have to tell and make believe. He let the woman beside him continue her long palaver about writing and her novel. He tried not to be irritated with the fact that a silly woman (she had become that suddenly) in his automobile was making small talk, while he sat there trying to comprehend that Gloria Wealdon was dead.

He tried to feel real remorse, but you never can right away. He felt just numb. He tried not to hope that this woman sitting beside him, by some miraculous and uncanny twist of fate, might be a crazy kind of godsend replacement for the client who had just died. (How had she died? He could not remember the strange man's voice on the phone saying how she had died; just that he was a friend of the Wealdons'; just that Gloria was dead.)

He wondered if Gloria had any more than a few chapters on the new book she had outlined (certainly not enough to matter?), and he was ashamed of himself for thinking of practical things. He knew that he would have another Martini, and then maybe another, and that he would probably read another chapter of this woman's manuscript. And he knew too that he did hope she was that never-happens-in-a-lifetime miracle, someone to step in out of the blue and fill the gap that existed now.

Still, sometimes a sudden death made sales rise, if it were unusually dramatic.

"Don't you think you ought to slow down?" said Edwina Dare.

But he hardly heard her say it.

Gloria Wealdon had earned for him well over thirty-five thousand dollars in less than a year.

Just remembering it so distracted Ralei that he almost ran into a small, green car parked alongside the highway.

Twenty-two

"I like surprises too," said Miles.
"Ah, but you're not the type that surprises happen to," Gina told him.
— FROM *Population 12,360*

"Whew!" the young woman in the green Volkswagen said. "I thought that fancy sportscar was going to wreck us. You," she said, poking her passenger's nose playfully with her finger, "and me," poking her own.

"I wouldn't let him."

"Wouldn't you?"

"No, I'd protect you, Rober."

"Why do you call me that?"

"I don't know."

"My name's Roberta."

"I know it."

"What if he *had* run into us?"

"I wouldn't let him."

"Say some more of those names."

"Really?"

"Yes."

"You like them?"

"I love them."

"All right, there's hardy candytuft."

"Hmmm."

"Catchfly campion."

"Hmmm."

"Oconee-bells."

"Nice!"

"Goldthread."

"Goldthread."

"Striped pipsissewa."

"That's a funny one."

"Twinflower."

"Umm-hmmm."

"Dwarf trillium."

"Dwarfs!" she giggled.

"Foamflower."

"Yes," she said.

"You don't want me to say any more, do you?"

"Why not?"

"Well, there's amur adonis, and prickly-thrift, and whit-low grass, and navelseed, and toadflax, and houseleek, and moonwort, and — "

"Moonwort! That's funny-funny."

"Moonwort," he said. "Moonwort."

"It's dark out."

"I know it is."

"Did you think this was going to happen to us today?"

"No," he lied.

"You didn't plan it, did you?"

"No," he lied again.

"Swear?"

"I swear," he said.

"I like it."

"What?"

"Being parked here, way away from nowhere."

"I do, too."

"Have you ever done it before?"

"No, Rober," he said honestly. "I never have."

"Do you have a guilty conscience?"

"No."

"'Course," she said, "why should you? We're just sitting here talking."

"Yes," he said. He put his arm around her.

She hiccuped.

"Excuse me."

"Certainly."

"They'll stop pretty soon."

"Yes."

"I hate hiccups."

"I'm the prince," he said, "and you're the little Cinderella. I'll stop your hiccups with a kiss."

He brushed his lips across her forehead. "You see?"

"Yes."

"They stopped, didn't they."

"Yes."

"We can thank St. Roque."

"Why?"

"He's the Saint of General Diseases."

"You know a lot, don't you? Nice things."

He smiled.

He said, "I hope you're not too hungry?"

Roberta Shagland cuddled into him.

She said, "I'm afraid that piece of coconut ice we shared has spoiled my appetite."

THE END

Vin Packer wrote many fine novels in the 50's and 60's, primarily for Gold Medal Books. They often tackled such topical subjects as sexual orientation and teenage alienation, and sold in the millions. Many of these novels were also superb works of suspense. In reality "Vin Packer" was Marijane Meaker, born in Auburn, New York, a graduate of The University of Missouri. She  retired the Packer pseudonym in 1966 and began writing a series of award-winning young adult novels as M. E. Kerr. She has also written novels under her own name, including the autobiographical *Highsmith, a Romance of the 50's*, a memoir of mystery writer Patricia Highsmith. She now lives in East Hampton, New York.

VIN PACKER BIBLIOGRAPHY

Novels:
Spring Fire (1952)
Dark Intruder (1952)
Look Back to Love (1953)
Come Destroy Me (1954)
Whisper His Sin (1954)
The Thrill Kids (1955)
The Young and Violent (1956)
Dark Don't Catch Me (1956)
3-Day Terror (1957)
5:45 to Suburbia (1958)
The Evil Friendship (1958)
The Twisted Ones (1959)
The Girl on the Bestseller List (1960)
The Damnation of Adam Blessing (1961)
Something in the Shadows (1961)
Intimate Victims (1962)
Alone at Night (1963)
The Hare in March (1966)
Don't Rely on Gemini (1969)

Stories:
Only the Guilty Run (*Ellery Queen's Mystery Magazine*, Oct 1955; *Some Things Weird and Wicked* edited by Joan Kahn, Pantheon, 1976)
Hot Snow (*Justice Magazine*, Jan 1956)
New York Will Break Your Heart, Baby (*Redbook*, Feb 1968)
Nothing Personal (*Redbook*, March 1969)
Jimmy from Another World (*Cosmopolitan*'s Winds of Love, Cosmopolitan Books, 1975)

As Ann Aldrich
We Walk Alone (1955)
We, Too, Must Love (1958)
Carol in a Thousand Cities [editor] (1960)
We Two Won't Last (1963)
Take a Lesbian to Lunch (1972)

As M. J. Meaker
A Guide to the Hangover (1962)
Sudden Endings (1964; reprinted in pb as by Vin Packer)
Hometown (1967)

As Marijane Meaker
Game of Survival (1968)
Shockproof Sydney Skate
  (1972)
Highsmith: A Romance of
  the 1950's (2003)
Scott Free (2007)

As M. E. Kerr
Dinky Hocker Shoots
  Smack (1972)
If I Love You, Am I
  Trapped Forever (1973)
The Son of Someone
  Famous (1974)
Is That You, Miss Blue?
  (1975)
Love is a Missing Person
  (1975)
I'll Love You When You're
  More Like Me (1977)
Gentlehands (1978)
Little Little (1981)
What I Really Think of
  You (1982)
Me Me Me Me Me: Not a
  Novel (1983)
Him She Loves? (1984)
I Stay Near You: One
  Story in Three (1985)

Night Kites (1986)
Fell (1987)
M. E. Kerr Introduces Fell
  (1988)
Fell Back (1989)
Fell Down (1991)
Linger (1993)
Deliver Us from Evie
  (1994)
"Hello" I Lied (1997)
Blood on the Forehead:
  What I Know About
  Writing (1998)
What Became of Her
  (2000)
Slap Your Sides (2001)
Snakes Don't Miss Their
  Mothers (2003)
Your Eyes in the Stars
  (2006)
Someone Like Summer
  (2009)

As Mary James
Shoebag (1991)
The Shuteyes (1993)
Frankenlouse (1994)
Shoebag Returns (1996)

Black Gat Books

Black Gat Books is a new line of mass market paperbacks introduced in 2015 by Stark House Press. New titles appear every three months, featuring the best in crime fiction reprints. Each book is sized to 4.25" x 7", just like they used to be. Collect them all!

Haven for the Damned by Harry Whittington
978-1-933586-75-5 $9.99

1 A group of eight people all converge on a small ghost town on the outskirts of the Mexican border, each with their own demons and dilemmas. They all want something they've lost: freedom, a lost wife, their youth. Not all of them will leave alive. May 2015.

Eddie's World by Charlie Stella
978-1-933586-76-2 $9.99

2 Charlie Stella's first great crime novel, back in print and available in paperback for the first time! Eddie Senta is suffering a mid-life crisis and decides to get involved in a heist. Everything that can go wrong, does. May 2015.

Stranger at Home by Leigh Brackett writing as George Sanders
978-1-933586-78-6 $9.99

3 Originally published as by the actor George Sanders, this domestic mystery by science fiction author Leigh Brackett is the story of a rich heel who comes back to get even with those who thought they had left him for dead. May 2015.

The Persian Cat by John Flagg
978-1933586-90-8 $9.99

4 A post-World War II thriller set in Teheran featuring cynical agent Gil Denby. His mission: bring a beautiful traitor to justice. His adversary: a major arms dealer. His odds: slim. August 2015.

Only the Wicked by Gary Phillips
978-1-933586-93-9 $9.99

5 The fourth Ivan Monk mystery, never before published in paperback. A tense Los Angeles thriller with roots in the Deep South. Author Sara Paretsky calls Phillips "my kind of crime writer and Ivan Monk is my kind of detective." November 2015.

Felony Tank by Malcolm Braly
978-1-933586-91-5 $9.99

6 Seventeen-year-old Doug is in the wrong place at the wrong time and ends up in jail. What happens next could only have been written by the author of *It's Cold Out There*. February 2016.

The Girl on the Bestseller List by Vin Packer
978-1-933586-98-4 $9.99

7 They all had a reason to hate Gloria Whealdon after she exposed their lives in her bestselling novel—but only one had a reason to kill. "I've read a number of Vin Packer's books, and this one remains a favorite."—*Bill Crider's Pop Culture Magazine*. May 2016.

She Got What She Wanted by Orrie Hitt
978-1-944520-04-5 $9.99

8 "This is a fine novel, sleaze paperback or literary, [on] how difficult it was for a woman not to have to resort to using her body and sexuality to get ahead in life." –Michael Hemmingson, *Those Sexy Vintage Sleaze Books*. August 2016.

Stark House Press

1315 H Street, Eureka, CA 95501
707-498-3135 * griffinskye3@sbcglobal.net
www.starkhousepress.com

Available from your local bookstore or direct from the publisher.